Forbidden Paths
of Thual

VICTOR KELLEHER

Forbidden Paths of Thual

with Decorations by
Antony Maitland

KESTREL BOOKS

KESTREL BOOKS
Published by Penguin Books Ltd
Harmondsworth, Middlesex, England

Copyright © 1979 by Victor Kelleher
Decorations Copyright © 1979 by Antony Maitland

First published 1979
ISBN 0 7226 5521 5
Printed in Great Britain by
Billing & Sons Ltd
Guildford, London and Worcester

Phototypeset in Great Britain by
Filmtype Services Limited, Scarborough

CONTENTS

1 · Decisions

QUEN awoke soon after dawn. The cool grey light creeping in through the doorway of the hut reminded him immediately of the Mollag. Instinctively, his mind went back to the day of their first coming: the arrival of their heavy grey ships on the nearby coast; the squat grey shapes lumbering ashore; their demands for some treasure or other which nobody had ever heard of. Give it up, they had said threateningly, or give up your freedom. But the people of the ten villages were poor. They possessed no such treasure. And so the Mollag had carried out their threat. How long ago that seemed now. Quen began slowly to count up the weeks . . . and then remembered his mother's stern warning. To carry the Mollag in your mind, she had said repeatedly, is to give them more than the treasure they seek. With an effort, he dismissed all thought of them and turned over on to his side.

The hut, which was a simple dome of willow and mud, had no windows. But from where he lay, he could look out through the low doorway at the huge towering trees of Thual, the great forest. Once it had reached right up to the edge of the village; and even now, after all the destruction, it began less than a quarter of a mile away, stretching into the distance as far as the eye could see, an endless plain of treetops. A holy place, very different from the Mollag. Again their long grey faces floated into his mind; and

7

again he struggled to dismiss them. What was it his mother had told the village? The threats of the Mollag were empty: the people of the ten villages were in the safekeeping of Thual, as they had always been. Nothing could harm the holy forest of Thual or those it protected.

That was an ancient truth which every child learned; and it worried Quen that he should begin to doubt it. To doubt the power of Thual and of the Pale Keepers who lived somewhere in its depths! Surely such thoughts were evil. As evil as the Mollag themselves. Yet why was it that the Mollag were allowed to do as they pleased? To enslave the people. To clear parts of the forest. To fell and drag out the tallest trees in order to build their towers. Why did the powers of Thual not turn on the grey invaders and drive them out?

These doubts had been pestering him for some time now, and in an attempt to overcome them he concentrated all his attention on the small portion of forest visible through the doorway. But on that particular morning, even Thual itself could do nothing to relieve his anxiety. The sun had not yet risen and the tall trees, with the tangle of undergrowth beneath, looked dark and brooding, as though waiting. But waiting for what? For the Mollag, those heavy grey figures he had come to fear? Or something else? Did the forest perhaps contain the treasure which the Mollag spoke of? And if so, where? For the hundredth time he realized that he could answer none of these questions. So that it was a relief when the doorway was suddenly darkened and his mother, stooping low, crept into the hut.

As the chief woman of the village, it was her task each morning to gather dry wood at the edge of the forest and to rekindle the village fire. She alone was allowed to do that because as a young girl, many years earlier, she had lived for a time deep within Thual, with the Pale Keepers. It was there that she had learned the secret power of the Eye.

On this, as on every other morning, she brought into the hut a rough earthenware pot filled with live coals. With these she lit their own small fire on which to cook the flat wheaten cakes which they ate for breakfast. Not until Quen could smell the smoke and see it drifting slowly up towards the hole

8

in the roof did he sit up and swing his feet down onto the floor.

His movements made the reed bed rustle, and his mother immediately turned towards him. Her face, as always, was smooth and calm; but her blue eyes, shadowed by dark brows, appeared troubled.

'Rest a while longer,' she said quietly. 'You will need all your strength for the journey ahead.'

He didn't understand her at first.

'But the Mollag have forbidden all journeys to other villages,' he said.

She shook her head.

'Not to another village.'

'Where then?'

'Into the forest of Thual.'

For a moment he thought he had misheard.

'But my journey . . .' he began, confused.

'I have told you,' she said sternly, 'your way lies into the forest.'

As she spoke, his father also crept into the hut. Quen could see from his face that he had heard his mother's words.

'Would you send our other child to his death as well?' he asked angrily. 'Is the loss of Arla not enough?'

At the mention of Arla, Quen glanced towards the empty reed bed beside his own, where his sister had slept until her arrest.

'Arla is not dead,' his mother said calmly. 'She has been imprisoned by the Mollag. You know that as well as I.'

'I also know,' Lod insisted, 'that the Mollag have threatened to kill her and many others unless we deliver the treasure they speak of.'

'That is true.'

'But we have no such treasure, Faya. And without it, do you honestly think they will ever release Arla alive?'

His mother lowered her eyes.

'I don't know,' she murmured.

'And yet you would send this boy into the forest,' his father said accusingly.

'It is the Mollag, not Thual, which have taken Arla from us,' his mother replied.

9

'But this will have the same result,' Lod said. 'He is not one of the Chosen. The Law of the Pale Keepers forbids his entering Thual. If they find him, who knows what they will do.'

Quen had never seen his parents disagree like this before. He knew that what Lod, his father, said was true. Lod did not possess the power of the Eye (none of the unchosen did), but he understood the Law as well as anyone in the ten villages. Quen, like his father, was surprised that his mother should even suggest that he should enter Thual, and he expected her now to give up the argument. But instead she opened her eyes wide and fixed his father with a stare which silenced him.

'Listen to me, Lod,' she said patiently. 'The time of the old Law is passing. It cannot help us against the Mollag – not if we do not help ourselves. That is why I wish to send Quen into the forest. I know that a grown man or woman, one of the unchosen, would never survive in there, would be soon hunted down. But a boy, not yet a man, might succeed where a man would fail.'

'That may be so,' his father agreed. 'But even supposing that he survives, what then? How long must he roam in there alone?'

'Ah,' his mother said quietly, 'it is not merely his survival which concerns me. Nor am I sending him to get help from the Pale Keepers. We have already seen that they cannot help us against the Mollag: not even the great power which they gave to Arla could save her from them. No, Quen's journey lies beyond the Pale Keepers, far beyond. His task,' and here she glanced at Quen, 'is to find the Wise Ones, the Keepers of the Great Eye.'

Quen saw on his father's face the same surprise which he felt himself.

'But nobody has ever seen them . . .' he stammered out, breaking in upon his parents.

'That is true,' Faya said. 'There has never been any reason to seek them out before. It has been enough to know they are there, the Guardians of the Eye. But now everything is different. We need their help. Because only the Great Eye, the root of their power, is capable of consuming the Mollag and of rescuing Thual and its people.'

'But why should Quen be the one to seek them out?' his father asked.

Faya answered patiently:

'Any grown person who leaves the ten villages will be missed immediately and tracked down by the Mollag. Whereas there is just a chance that a child's absence will be overlooked or ignored, that the Mollag will not think him worth following. Add to that the fact that Quen is small and quick, capable of moving unseen through the forest. With courage and some luck he might escape both the Mollag and the Pale Keepers.'

Lod nodded his agreement and Faya again looked towards her son.

'What do you say, Quen?' she asked. 'Will you undertake such a journey?'

Quen was aware of his mother's powers. She had no need to ask for his consent. She had only to fix him with her eyes and he would have no choice but to do her bidding. Yet her eyes were narrowed, her heavy dark lashes veiling the deep blue. He realized instantly that she did not wish to force him: she wished him to make a free choice.

When he hesitated, she added:

'The journey will be dangerous. And I can give you no instructions or maps – only two ancient sayings passed on to me by my grandmother. The first of them is this: that the Wise Ones are hidden in the Eye. And the second: that the Sacred Eye can be grasped, but never possessed. What they mean, I cannot say, but they may be of some use to you later.'

Still without answering, he looked towards his father for guidance: but Lod remained silent. Quen thought, if only Arla were here to advise me. And straight away the idea of Arla reminded him powerfully of the Mollag, their sinister grey presence occupying the land. For a moment, the sharp metallic smell of their bodies seemed to fill the hut, as on the morning when they had come and taken Arla. And in the instant of recalling that morning, his decision was made.

'You are sure that the Sacred Eye will consume them?' he asked.

'We are told,' she said quietly, 'that all evil is consumed by it.'

'Then I shall go,' he replied.

2 · Preparations

THROUGHOUT the cooking and eating of their simple breakfast, Quen and his parents said little. Only after the hut had been tidied and the fire covered with light ash to preserve it during the day did Faya break the silence.

'The bronze bell will soon be rung,' she said. 'We must prepare you for your journey.'

'Must I leave now?' he asked. 'In daylight?'

She nodded.

'But how will I pass the Mollag guard and enter the forest?'

'You will come with us to the fields as on every other morning,' she explained. 'We will work close to the edge of the forest, as far from the towers as possible. The guards cannot watch all the time. As soon as they are careless, you will step in between the trees.'

'You mean you will send him into Thual unarmed?' his father asked.

'If the Pale Keepers were to find him armed,' she answered, 'the punishment would be severe. Nobody may carry weapons in Thual. You know that.'

'But the Pale Keepers are not the only danger,' Lod objected. 'There are also the Mollag who are already scouting in the forest and who may well follow him. He must have some defence against them.'

'I agree,' Faya said, 'but his main defence must be speed. With luck, they will not notice his absence for a day or even two. By then he should be far from here.'

'That is not defence enough,' Lod argued. 'How can speed alone help him against creatures who never sleep, who can travel tirelessly day and night? What will he do to defend himself if they are close behind him, hunting him down?'

'He will then have to rely on his cunning,' Faya said. 'The Mollag are creatures of habit, Quen is not.'

This time, however, Lod remained unconvinced by her arguments.

'No,' he said firmly. 'I have agreed to the journey, but I cannot agree to this. If he is to set out at all, it must be at night. And he must be armed.'

Quen expected his mother to use the power of the Eye to make his father agree. Lod, too, must have expected it because he kept his head lowered. But once again Faya chose not to use her power.

'In this,' she said, 'we must all be of one mind. What is your opinion, Quen?'

She turned towards her son.

He hesitated for a moment, imagining to himself the actual journey: the cool green paths, like tunnels through the forest; the dark eerie nights full of strange and threatening sounds; the unknown beasts lying in the undergrowth; and finally the Mollag themselves.

'I'd prefer to go armed,' he said.

'Then it must be at night,' Faya decided, 'when you can slip past the guards completely unseen.'

Before she finished speaking, the bronze bell began to ring from the camp tower. Quen was about to reach for the hoe he used in the fields when Faya stopped him.

'If you are to travel by night,' she said, 'you must rest throughout the day. I shall tell the guards you are ill. That way they may not notice your absence tomorrow.'

Already, outside, the Mollag guards were shouting commands

13

in their clipped metallic speech, and Lod and Faya gathered up their tools and went out. For a while there was a general noise of people milling around near the centre of the village. But it didn't last for long. The Mollag hated to waste time and within minutes the work parties had all been marched off, leaving the village silent and empty.

Left to himself, Quen lay back on the reed bed. He felt too excited by what had happened to be able to sleep. Also, his head was full of the adventure which awaited him. But he closed his eyes just the same and tried to rest; and slowly, as the morning wore on, he fell into a fitful, dreamy sleep.

At about midday he was suddenly snapped awake by a noise somewhere in the village. It took him only a matter of seconds to realize what was happening. The regular heavy tread and the harsh clash of leather and bronze told him clearly that a Mollag guard was checking the village, making sure that nobody was hiding from the work parties. Quen listened intently as the heavy footsteps moved from hut to hut, coming gradually closer. All too soon they had reached the adjoining hut; and then they were moving directly towards where he lay. He remained quite still, steeling himself for the encounter, knowing that he would be beaten as soon as it was discovered he was not ill. But just as the thick leather boots appeared in the low doorway, his mother's voice rang out sharply:

'I've already told you. The boy is ill and sleeping.'

The reply was in a harsh toneless voice, a sound not unlike the jagged rasping of a file on metal.

'Be silent, woman, and get back to the fields. I have come here to see for myself, not to listen to your lies.'

'Truly, I am not lying,' she said humbly. 'He is ill, with a fever. If you go in, you will only wake him and make the fever worse.'

Her voice sounded different from normal, unnaturally loud, as though she were trying to tell him something. But what? What was it she had said? A fever! With sudden inspiration Quen glanced round the hut. The large earthen water pot was in its usual place, not far from the head of his bed. Carefully, so as to make no noise, he reached out, scooped up a palmful of water, and dabbed it onto his forehead and cheeks and neck. Then he closed his eyes and waited.

There was a scraping of coarse leather in the doorway, and suddenly the hut was full of a heavy choking smell. Quen's instinct was to roll away, to hide his face against the mud wall; but he forced himself to remain still, eyes closed, breathing regularly. With a touch like ice, the cold three-fingered hand felt his forehead and groped clumsily at his neck, searching for a pulse. A moment later, there was a hard satisfied grunt and the noise of the creature leaving the hut.

As soon as he was alone, Quen opened his eyes. For the time being he was safe: clearly the Mollag had mistaken the water for sweat and the fearful beating of his heart for a sign of sickness. Just the same, Quen felt shaken, and also unclean, soiled by the cold touch of the three-fingered hand. He had not opened his eyes to see, but he could visualize it perfectly: the blunt grey-blue nails set into the dead flesh of the fingers like scoops of dull metal. With a shudder, he filled a small bowl with water and washed his face and neck thoroughly. That made him feel better, yet for several hours afterwards he continued to recall that icy touch and for the remainder of the day he found it impossible to sleep.

His parents returned from the fields just before sunset. Although they were both tired from the long hours of work, Faya began to cook their evening meal immediately. While she worked, Lod helped his son prepare his weapons. In theory, the possession of arms was strictly forbidden by the Mollag, but in fact almost every household had weapons hidden away. Together, Lod and Quen moved the reed beds and dug down into the earth floor to where their own secret store was hidden. Quen chose a short, light bow made of carved wood and a quiver of thin arrows – together they weighed no more than a pound or two and would not slow him down. For a hand weapon he selected a flat-bladed sword, only slightly longer than a large knife, which hung from a leather scabbard at his side. Lod also wanted him to carry a spear, but he refused, saying it would prevent his moving easily and quickly through the underbrush. Instead, he took a small, delicately bladed knife which fitted snugly down the inside of his boot and could not be seen.

By the time they had smoothed the earth floor and replaced the beds, it was almost dark outside and the food was ready. They ate quickly, knowing that every second now was valuable. Quen, especially, felt driven by a sense of urgency and only minutes after the meal he was dressed in a short woollen tunic, the sword strapped to his side, the bow and quiver slung across his back so that his hands were free. As the last of the daylight faded and the shadows around the forest thickened, he crouched beside the low doorway ready to leave.

But at the last moment, Faya stopped him.

'There is one thing I wish you to take with you,' she said.

Around her neck was a thin leather cord; and attached to this cord, but hidden by her clothing, was a small cloth bag. She pulled out the bag and took something from it, something tiny and fragile which she cradled in the palm of her hand. Quen leaned forward to discover what it was and saw a glittering round stone, smaller than his thumbnail, but perfectly formed, a point of brilliant light in the gloomy interior of the hut.

'It is a diamond,' Faya said, 'a sacred stone given to me by the Pale Keepers. Carry it with you. It is your sign, proof that you come in the name of the ten villages.'

Swiftly she put it back in the small protective bag, slipped the bag from the cord, and gave it to Quen who hid it in the inside pocket of his tunic.

By then, it was dark outside, a warm moonless night without wind. There was no longer any reason to delay and Quen turned to his father. Lod's face was anxious and troubled, but he showed none of his emotion in his voice.

'Go well, my son,' he said gruffly, placing one hand briefly on his son's shoulder.

Faya, too, showed none of her deep feelings.

'May Thual shelter and protect you,' she said quietly.

She reached out and brushed Quen's cheek lightly with her fingertips, then stepped back. And in a single movement, Quen ducked through the low doorway and was gone.

3 · Setting Out

OUTSIDE, it was quiet and breathless, the stillness broken only by the subdued noises of the village and by the occasional cry of an owl in the forest. After the first few paces, Quen stopped and crouched low to the ground. For several minutes he didn't move, allowing his eyes to accustom themselves to the near darkness. Slowly, the details of the narrow plain emerged from the gloom: the round, huddled shapes of the huts; the fresh furrows of newly tilled land; the black, brooding line of the forest; and finally the gaunt outline of the wooden towers.

He knew that the towers were placed three hundred yards apart and that there was one Mollag soldier to each tower. At regular intervals, each of these soldiers left his tower and patrolled a section of the plain. What Quen had to do was to wait for the patrol to pass and then to creep noiselessly into the forest.

Drawing a deep breath, he moved slowly forward, still crouched low, to a point nearly two hundred yards from the village. Again he stopped and waited, listening for even the slightest noise. For some time, nothing moved around him; and then, faintly to begin with, he detected the slow even tread of the guard. Lying down full length in the deep furrow, Quen peered into the darkness. He could just make out the dim outline of the creature as it walked slowly away from the nearest tower, turned, and walked back. Not until the Mollag had disappeared back into the darkness did Quen rise and move towards the forest.

Running lightly on the soft earth, he made hardly any sound and he was confident of reaching the trees unseen. But just before he drew level with the towers, his foot suddenly tripped against something thin and hard which sent him sprawling forwards onto his hands and knees. Even as he fell, Quen realized what had happened: the Mollag had stretched a wire between the towers to prevent precisely this kind of escape. Immediately a light flared in the nearest tower and a hard voice called into the darkness.

Jumping to his feet, Quen sprinted towards the shelter of the trees. He was a fast runner and had every chance of out-distancing the tower guard. But when he was only yards from safety, another squat figure stepped out of the forest and barred his way. Instinctively, Quen tried to dodge past, but the creature was armed with a long spear which it thrust out towards him, preventing his escape.

'Stand where you are,' the guard said.

Slowly, Quen backed away, keeping just out of range of the jabbing spear. To run back, he knew, would be useless: the guard would easily recognize him again; and in any case, his task was to reach the forest. But how? As he hesitated, he heard behind him the sound of running feet, followed immediately by the noise of an armed struggle. While he was still wondering what was happening, Faya suddenly appeared out of the darkness, breathless but unharmed.

'Lod is keeping the other guards at bay,' she panted out. 'Now is your only chance.'

And turning to the single Mollag soldier, she opened her eyes wide and fixed him with her stare. He had been about to advance on them, his spear held at the ready. But now he stopped, frozen in his tracks, the round black pools of his eyes gazing sightlessly into space.

'Now!' Faya said fiercely. 'Run, Quen, run!'

'But what about Lod . . . ?' he began.

She cut him off with a wave of the hand.

18

'Lod is giving you this time! Don't waste it! Run, now!'

Miserably, he circled around the motionless guard and entered the black leafy shadows of Thual. But instead of running deeper into the forest, he turned and crouched in the waist-high ferns. From there he could still see Faya: she had not taken her eyes from the guard who remained frozen in the same position. In the distance, the noise of fighting had stopped. Quen heard Lod let out a half-stifled cry of warning and seconds later another Mollag guard came lumbering out of the night behind Faya.

As fast as he could, Quen unslung the bow and fitted an arrow to it; but before he could draw back the string, the guard had reached his mother and struck her down with the side of his shield. Immediately, the first Mollag soldier jerked awake and spun around to glare into the forest. Somewhere in the back of his mind, Quen knew that now, more than ever, he should try to escape. At the same time he felt choked with rage at what they had done to Faya. Pulling the string back full stretch, he shot straight at the thick outline of the second guard. There was a dull clang as the arrow-head glanced uselessly off the smooth body armour. That steadied him, and the next arrow was more considered, aimed at the knee, one of the few weak points in the Mollag's protective clothing. But in that poor light it was a difficult shot and the thud of the arrow striking leather told him he had missed his mark and merely hit the thick legging.

After that there was no time for another shot. Both guards had pulled their shields up in front of them and together they came charging into the forest.

Quen had no choice now but to turn and run. By pure chance he stumbled onto one of the narrow curving paths and scurried down it, bent forward to avoid the overhanging branches. For the first few minutes he gained steadily on the guards who came crashing through the undergrowth behind him. He had no intention of escaping altogether, however; once he was well clear of them, he stopped and lay down in the ferns a few feet to the side of the path. It took only a minute or two for the guards to reach him. They came lumbering towards where he lay, jabbing sword and spear into the earth on either side of them as they ran. Quen had not expected that, and the long spear-head which had

19

threatened him earlier now narrowly missed his cheek and made a thin slice across the point of his shoulder. Had he called out, he would instantly have been captured; but he somehow stifled the cry of surprise and pain, and the guards, unaware that he was there, ran on into the forest.

As soon as they were well past him, Quen hurried back towards Faya. She was sitting up when he reached her, the side of her face bruised and swollen from the blow of the shield.

'You should be far from here by now!' she said angrily as soon as she saw him.

'I had to find out if you were safe,' he explained.

'I *am* all right,' she said impatiently.

'And Lod?'

She rose slowly and painfully to her feet, staggering a little from dizziness.

'I shall try to help Lod,' she said more gently. 'Your sole concern now must be to find the Sacred Eye. Only in that way can you bring true and lasting safety to any of us.'

While she was speaking, Quen's keen hearing detected the noise of the returning guards.

'Have no fears for my safety,' Faya added. 'I can defend myself and also delay them long enough for you to strike deep into the forest. Now go!'

With surprising strength, she turned him forcibly around and pushed him towards the trees. Reluctantly, he re-entered the forest, ran on for thirty or forty paces, and again stopped. He felt torn by indecision, unsure whether to begin his long journey or stay and help his mother and father. As he stood there undecided, the guards came pounding back, passing close by where he waited. There was a snarl of rage as they burst out into the clearing, followed by a babble of unintelligible speech. Quen had half-turned, already reaching for another arrow to fit into the bow, when he heard the unmistakable screech of a Mollag in pain. After that there was total silence.

But now, at last, Quen was decided; and slinging the bow onto his back once again, he ran off into the trackless darkness of Thual.

4 · Flight

AFTER the first few hundred yards Quen made no attempt to hurry. The path on which he found himself was narrow and twisting, with bushes and branches constantly blocking his way, so that in the darkness he had to move carefully in order to avoid falling or making too much noise. Also, he remembered what his father had said: how the Mollag could travel tirelessly day and night. There was no point in running fast and exhausting himself in the first hour. The best thing was to conserve his energy; and with that in mind he settled into a steady jogging run which, if necessary, he could keep up for many hours.

There had been no rain for several weeks and the ground was hard, which meant that provided he made no noise, there was little chance of his being tracked at night. Even so, he was on the lookout for a stream or river and felt relieved when the ground began to slope gradually downwards. By then, the moon had risen and was casting a faint ghostly light through the trees. The light helped him find his way, but also increased his nervousness. Before, he had been merely lost in the darkness: now, the dim outline of the huge trees made him feel tiny and alone, like a dwarf in the overgrown garden of some vast giant.

He had meant to keep moving until he reached water; but the

wound in his shoulder began to worry him and he stopped briefly in a patch of moonlight to examine it. The cut itself was not deep: normally, it would have given him little trouble. But the constant jolting as he ran had prevented the cut from closing, with the result that it had continued to bleed steadily.

Obviously something had to be done, otherwise he would begin to lose strength from loss of blood. Crouching down on the narrow pathway, he tried to think, and immediately he became aware of the eerie silence of Thual. For a split second he almost panicked as all the stories he had ever heard about the forest crowded in upon him. In that brief moment, the trees themselves seemed to move in towards him, great menacing shapes which threatened to crush him to death, to bury him in gloom and silence forever. He wanted to cry out for help, from anyone, and had actually opened his mouth to call, when suddenly, just above his head, an owl hooted; and at that familiar sound which he had heard all his life, the feeling of panic disappeared as quickly as it had come, leaving his mind fresh and clear. Without any further hesitation, he tore a strip of cloth from the soft quiver which held his arrows and tied it as best he could around his shoulder. It eased the sharp ache slightly, and again he moved on.

Now the ground sloped more steeply than ever, and within half an hour he came to a small river which wound slowly through the forest. This was what he had been hoping for, because it gave him the chance to cover his tracks completely. Treading carefully so as not to dislodge any stones, he waded in until he was out of his depth. The cool water stung his injured shoulder, but he ignored the pain, concentrating on keeping afloat, allowing the current to carry him steadily downstream.

He floated like that for some time, resisting the temptation to reach up to the many branches which hung out over the river. Not until he had travelled nearly a mile did he grasp one of the thicker limbs and hoist himself clear of the water. The effort sent sharp pains through his shoulder, but again he ignored the discomfort; and clenching his teeth, he pulled himself right up into the tree.

His task now was to keep clear of the ground for as long as possible. With increasing difficulty, he clambered from tree to tree, walking out along swaying branches, swinging dangerously high above the ground, snatching at widespread leafy boughs which bent and creaked under his weight. His progress was slow, but he knew the time was well spent because when he finally climbed to the ground he was well clear of the river.

This meant that the Mollag could not track him merely by crossing the river and following its course until they picked up his footprints. To discover precisely where he had left the water, they would have to search a very wide area indeed. Given time, of course, they would probably pick up his prints once again; but then time was what Quen needed above all else.

After a brief rest he again continued his journey, keeping his eye on the moon and working his way always steadily east. For a while he felt chilled by his wet tunic; but the constant movement soon warmed him and he fell once more into a slow plodding rhythm, covering the miles at a steady pace. On several occasions in the hours that followed there were sudden noises in the undergrowth, followed by the sound of heavy animals crashing away through the trees. Each time that happened, Quen's heart leaped into his mouth. Nonetheless, he rarely stopped, and then only to rest his aching shoulder or to readjust the crude bandage.

As the night wore on, the shoulder wound worried him more. The ache became worse, and although the bleeding was very slight, it wouldn't stop. He had decided earlier that he would keep moving until dawn; but in the last few hours of darkness he was forced to rest repeatedly. And when dawn finally did begin to lighten the eastern sky, he felt dizzy and sick.

He slowed down to a mere walk now, knowing that he could not keep going much longer. As the growing light of day gradually filtered through into the green gloom of Thual, he looked around him keenly, searching for a safe place to rest. He found it at last, just as the first rays of the sun touched the topmost branches high above his head. It was a huge wild fig tree, its trunk wider than a large hut, its roots coiling and spreading above ground in all directions. Beneath the roots there was a network of tunnels and holes, and it was into one of these tunnels that Quen crawled.

Ahead of him, in the darkness, an animal snarled and slunk

23

away; but Quen was too tired and ill to care. Crawling on hands and knees, he came to the animal's still warm nest, and curling up in it himself he fell instantly into a deep sleep.

He awoke later in the day, much later than he had intended, and realized instantly that he was seriously ill. He was burning hot, and when he sat up the world seemed to sway and dip all around him. His shoulder, which had swollen while he slept, was too sore even to touch, and the slightest movement of his arm sent pains shooting up into his body.

With great difficulty, using only his right hand to support himself, he began to crawl along the musty tunnel towards the daylit forest. But almost immediately, he stopped. Where he had slept, two tunnels crossed; and looking down one of these, he was startled to see the leather-clad legs of a Mollag soldier. Even the few movements Quen had made had attracted the soldier's attention, and he knelt down and peered in under the tree. Quen froze in the darkness, not daring to move. The soldier was not more than ten feet from where he lay: Quen could see clearly the flat round discs of the eyes, the open up-turning nostrils, the short thick horns which curved across the creature's forehead. For perhaps a full minute the soldier remained crouching there, then he grunted, rose, and walked slowly away.

Quen realized that the safest thing to do was to remain where he was. He could not be seen from outside and it was doubtful whether the thick-set Mollag soldier could squeeze himself along the narrow tunnels between the roots. On the other hand, Quen was burning with fever and had to reach water soon. Also, if the soldier was really suspicious, there was the chance that he would use fire to smoke Quen out. In a moment Quen's mind was made up, and taking as much care as possible, he began to inch his way towards the circle of daylight.

When he reached it, the guard was nowhere to be seen. Slowly, Quen crawled out into the day and stood up. The effort made him feel sick, and for a second or two he almost passed out. Somehow he managed not to fall. Gripping tightly with both hands, he fought off the heaving dizziness which threatened to draw him down into a whirlpool of darkness. Gradually the ground under his feet, which had seemed to swing dangerously, settled and grew still; and when he came fully to himself he found he was leaning on one of the curved roots and staring at the heavily armoured back of the Mollag soldier. The creature, unaware of Quen, was standing on the other side of the tree, head bent, leaning on a wooden club.

Momentarily, all Quen's feelings of sickness left him. Ducking down, he backed quietly away, turned, and slipped unseen through the bushes. While he was still within earshot he walked quietly and carefully; but once he was a safe distance from the tree he broke into a staggering run. He could not keep it up, and after less than half a mile he stumbled to a halt and leaned gasping against a tree.

For some time he could hear nothing but the frantic pounding of his own heart. When that had quietened and he had caught his breath, he sank down on the mossy ground to rest and to assess his position. But not for long. His instincts and his keen hearing soon told him that this particular part of the forest was alive with Mollag soldiers. He heard the heavy tramp of their feet somewhere over to the left; and a little later, the jabber of their harsh mechanical voices deeper in the forest.

He rose unsteadily, wondering which way to turn, and caught the faint sound of someone behind him. He whirled around and saw a vague movement among the bushes. Could it have been a bird or an animal? Or the Mollag soldier following from the tree? Without waiting to find out, he hurried away along the path.

In the hour that followed, he had little idea of where he was going. He half-ran, half-walked, stumbling along, dizzy and confused. More and more frequently, he had to pause and rest; and each time that he stopped, he heard the same faint sound behind him, saw the same vague movement in the bushes. In his confusion he could not work out why the soldier didn't simply run him down. Once or twice the thought crossed his mind that the Mollag were perhaps tormenting him, hunting him to a standstill as they might a deer or hare; but he was too ill and tired to concentrate on that idea for long. He needed all his concentration merely to keep going; and every time he heard the faint sound behind him he drove himself closer to exhaustion.

Finally, when he could hardly stand, least of all walk or run, he saw ahead of him the familiar outline of a large tree. Leaving the path, he stumbled through the ferns and bushes and burst out into the small clearing which he had left only an hour earlier. Before him was the giant fig tree with its twisting, curving roots; and in front of the tree, leering at him, was the Mollag soldier he had fled from. In a flash, Quen realized that he had travelled in a complete circle. He looked back and again caught the hint of movement behind him. He thought, I'm trapped; and with a sinking heart he turned back to face the tree. The Mollag soldier was preparing to run at him, the club raised above his head. With his last strength, Quen drew his short sword and made ready to meet the attack. But this last effort was too much for him: his whole world tilted and slipped sideways, the sky and trees whirling and spiralling above him. Something sailed past his head, and as he passed out, it seemed to his dazed eyes as if he were dragging the Mollag soldier with him, the two of them toppling together, sliding down towards the darkening earth.

5 · The Woodsman

HE opened his eyes and looked up. About six feet above his head was a rough ceiling of black rock which curved down towards a floor of beaten earth. Even without sitting up, he could tell that he was lying in a cave. Just the same, he propped himself up on one elbow and looked around. Behind him, there was a jagged opening in the rock wall; and beyond the opening, a narrow flight of stone steps leading upwards. Faint sunlight fell onto the steps, but failed to enter the cave which was dim and cool. Somewhere above him he could hear the sounds of bird calls and the wind rustling the leaves of Thual.

How he came to be in such a place, Quen could not even begin to guess; and swinging his feet down onto the earth floor, he sat up and took stock of his situation. The bed on which he had slept was similar to his own at home – a low wooden bench heaped high with soft dry reeds. Someone must have put him on it. But who? And probably that same person had taken off his tunic and cleaned and dressed the wound on his shoulder. Thankfully, he flexed his shoulder and discovered that most of the pain had gone. It was still stiff and sore, but was clearly beginning to heal. He knew from experience that more than just a few hours were needed for such healing to take place and he suddenly began to wonder how long he had been lying there in the cave.

Gathering his strength, he rose shakily to his feet. All his fever had gone and although he felt weak and slightly light-headed, he was well enough. He noticed that in the far corner of the cave, on a crude wooden bench, were all his belongings: his tunic and boots and his few weapons – which meant that whatever else his unknown helper might be, he was no thief. Or was he? Hurrying unsteadily across the cave, Quen picked up the tunic and felt in the inner pocket for the small cloth bag containing the diamond which Faya had given him. It was gone! Hopelessly, he searched amongst the rest of his belongings; but it was nowhere to be found.

Quen had very little idea of why Faya had given him the stone. Yet he remembered her words when she had handed it to him. 'Carry it with you,' she had said. 'It is your sign.' His sign! Like his own name, or the distinctive markings on the palm of his hand. Obviously she would not have used such a word unless the stone was important; and at the thought of his loss Quen felt overcome by misery. It seemed for a moment that his journey was over almost before it had begun, and with a sigh he sank down onto the wooden bench.

He didn't stay like that for long: the light in the cave was already beginning to fail and it occurred to him that the thief, whoever he was, had left him there to fend for himself. Taking care not to disturb the dressing on his shoulder, he slipped his tunic back on. Yet no sooner had he done so than there was a sound of footsteps behind him. Moving quickly, he pulled his sword from its sheath and backed against the wall. A moment later, a man came down the stone steps and paused in the doorway. He was tall and lean, obviously very strong, dressed in soft woollen trousers and jacket, and shoes which appeared to be made from the bark of a tree. He was no longer young, though not yet old, his hair black and shoulder length, his beard streaked with grey.

'So you have woken at last,' he said quietly.

'And while I slept,' Quen said accusingly, 'someone has taken my stone.'

'*Your* stone?' the man asked. 'Was it ever yours to lose?'

'Yes, mine!' Quen cried.

The man shook his head doubtfully; and walking across the cave, he swung the short stick he was carrying and knocked the sword effortlessly from Quen's hand. Then, ignoring Quen's futile struggles, he picked him up and carried him back to the reed bed.

'Only one of the Chosen may possess such a stone,' he said. 'And that does not include you. The Chosen do not number amongst the children of violence; they do not carry weapons. They would never enter Thual, as you have done, armed with steel and bow. Therefore let me ask you again – to whom does this stone truly belong?'

'Who are you to ask such questions?' Quen said.

'I? My name is Nodak. I am a woodsman. I ask you in the name of Thual. And if you know anything of this forest, you will understand that it is better and safer for you to give your answers to me than to the Pale Keepers.'

'You will learn nothing by threatening me,' Quen replied.

'What I have told you is not a threat, but a fact. The Pale Keepers do not treat kindly those who have no place here.'

What Nodak said was so obviously true that Quen gave up the argument. He was impressed by Nodak's gentle manner and by the realization that it was probably he who had cleaned his wound and cared for him.

'All right,' Quen said. 'But first tell me how I came to be here.'

'That is easily told,' Nodak replied. 'I first saw you in the forest when you were fleeing from the Mollag. It is not my duty to guide those who come armed into Thual and so I merely followed you. Only when you fainted and were defenceless against the Mollag soldier did I step between you. Also, I was curious to discover why so many of them should be hunting you.'

As he spoke, Quen's memory of his journey came flooding back. For the first time he looked closely at the thick stick which Nodak grasped lightly in his hands.

'That stick,' he said, 'was that what came whirling past my head just as I was falling?'

'Yes, the Mollag also slept. Not for long; but long enough for me to pick you up and carry you to safety. You had a bad fever: you have been lying here for three days and nights.'

'Then I owe you my life,' Quen said.

Nodak shrugged.

'Perhaps.'

'In that case,' Quen answered, 'the least I can do is tell you the truth. My mother is one of the Chosen. It is she who sent me into the forest, in order to find the Wise Ones, the Guardians of the Sacred Eye. Before I left, she gave me the stone.'

'And the weapons?'

'They were my father's idea . . . and mine,' he added.

'Why have they sent you on this mission?' Nodak asked.

'It is because of the Mollag. They arrived in long boats several months ago. They said they had come for a treasure which we possess. But nobody in the ten villages has any knowledge of it. Since then they have enslaved the people and chopped down the trees of Thual in order to build their towers and clear ground for their crops. No one can drive them out. Not even the Pale Keepers – who sent my sister Arla, one of the Chosen, back to the village to help us. There has never been anybody who possessed the power of the Eye as much as she. I have seen her still five guards with a single glance. But now they have taken even her. They say that without the treasure they will never leave our shores.'

Nodak remained silent and thoughtful for several minutes.

'Your task is a difficult one,' he murmured at last. 'It is said that the Wise Ones are hidden within the Eye itself.'

'That is what my mother told me,' Quen said.

'And what else did she tell you?'

'That the Eye can be grasped, but never possessed.'

Nodak nodded his agreement.

'That, too, I have heard before.'

'Then you perhaps know where the Wise Ones are to be found?' Quen asked excitedly.

'Ah, only the Wise Ones themselves know that,' Nodak replied. 'I have also heard it said that in order to know them, a person must first come to share some of their wisdom. And I . . . I am a simple woodsman. All I am certain of is this: that it is the duty of all men to protect Thual; for without the forest, there would be . . . nothing.'

While they had been speaking, it had grown almost dark in the cave. Nodak left Quen alone for a short time and returned with a small lamp, two bowls, and an earthen pot containing warm stew. The smell of the stew made Quen feel suddenly ravenous and he watched expectantly as Nodak filled the two bowls. When he received his portion, he dug eagerly to the bottom of the bowl, searching for meat. But he found none – only roots and berries and fungi from the forest. He made no comment about it at the time; and not for several days did he think of it again.

The immediate effect of the meal was to make Quen feel heavy and drowsy.

'You are still weak,' Nodak said. 'Now it is better to sleep than to talk' – and he took the bowls and pot outside.

There were still many things Quen wished to ask him; but left to himself he found it impossible to stay awake. He decided to doze off for just a few minutes and he closed his eyes. But when he awoke, the night had gone, it was broad daylight, and Nodak was standing silently in the cave watching him.

'You are stronger today,' the tall woodsman said softly. 'I can see it in your face.'

Quen sat up and stretched, moving his shoulder freely now.

'I must thank you for healing my wound,' he said.

Nodak dismissed the thanks with a movement of his hands.

'That is nothing – no more than my duty. I would do the same for any other creature of the forest. Much more important – what I have been thinking about while you were asleep – is why so many Mollag soldiers should go to the trouble of hunting down one boy. You spoke last night of a treasure which the Mollag seek. Could it be that they are convinced you are the key to the treasure? Do they perhaps believe that you know of the treasure's whereabouts?'

Quen had not thought of that possibility. Now, for the first time, he considered it. He tried to put himself in the Mollag's place. How would they have seen his escape? Just as a young boy running from a village? But then why had he gone so deep into the forest, which for most of the villagers was a forbidden place? And why had both of his parents risked their lives in order to help him on his way? Yes, from their point of view, it certainly looked suspicious. Add to that the fact that the Mollag were convinced of the treasure's existence and . . ..

'You may be right,' Quen said. 'But if they suspect that I know where the treasure is, why don't they simply follow me? That would require only a few trackers. Whereas it seems from all the soldiers that were in the forest that they mean to capture me.'

'It presents a problem,' Nodak said, 'only if you ignore the Mollag themselves, what they are. They are things of greed: it is not in their nature to play a passive, following game. When they see something, they must possess it, hold it instantly in their hands. If they truly believe you are the key to the treasure, then it is far more likely that they should try to capture you and torture the information out of you. That is their way.'

Quen could not deny that what Nodak said made grim sense.

'Which means,' Nodak went on, 'that not just your freedom, but your life is in danger. Because if they catch you, they will carry their torture through to death.'

The situation which Nodak presented was not a pleasant one. He was saying in effect that what had begun as a journey was now a hunt to the death – with Quen as victim. To bolster his own courage, Quen got up from the bed and went over to where his weapons lay at the ready.

As though reading his mind, Nodak said:

'I have told you before: it is forbidden to carry arms in the forest of Thual.'

Quen laid his hand on the hilt of the sword for reassurance.

'Will you try to prevent my taking these?' he said threateningly.

'No,' Nodak answered mildly, 'that is not my wish. I would merely remind you of what you already know: that the forest is sacred, as is everything in it. No living creature may harm or kill another unless it is absolutely necessary. To kill is to destroy the eternal balance which is Thual itself.'

'Yet the Mollag seek to kill and destroy,' Quen argued, 'and neither you nor anyone else does a thing to stop them.'

'That is because they contain within themselves the seeds of their own extinction,' Nodak explained carefully. 'They are typical hunters: they are aware of nothing but their own greed.

32

Compared with the timid deer, or even the tiny squirrels in the trees, they are blind and deaf. They hear nothing; they see nothing; they smell nothing. The glory that is Thual is hidden from them. Their monstrous greed, like a whip, lashes them on to destruction.'

'And have I no right to defend myself against these monsters?' Quen asked angrily.

'There are many ways of defending yourself. If you choose to carry weapons, you become no better than the Mollag. For like them you will be ready and able to kill – the temptation will always be there in your hands.'

He finished speaking and turned towards the door of the cave.

'Before you go,' Quen said, 'there is one other thing: my stone; I wish to have it back.'

Nodak paused in the doorway.

'The Pale Keepers do not give their gems away,' he said quietly. 'They believe that such stones must first be earned.'

'That may be true,' Quen replied. 'Still, it is mine, and I wish to have it.'

'If it is truly yours, you shall,' Nodak said, and he disappeared silently up the steps.

Quen remained in the cave, feeling angry and cheated. He sat down on the bed, thinking of all the things he would say when Nodak came back. But the minutes passed and no returning footsteps were heard. A new and disturbing idea occurred to Quen.

'Nodak!' he called urgently, 'Nodak!'

There was no reply. With sudden alarm, Quen climbed unsteadily up the stairs. On the top step, where he could not possibly overlook it, was a small heap of nuts and berries. Stepping over them, he walked out onto a rock shelf and found himself on a low hill overlooking the forest. Nobody was visible on the bare rocky slope, and apart from the gentle swaying of the treetops and the lazy circling of a hawk high above him, there was no movement anywhere. With a sudden sinking feeling, Quen realized that the stone was gone and that he was completely alone once more.

6 · The Hunter and the Hunted

ALTHOUGH all his instincts told him that Nodak had gone, Quen did not leave the rocky hill immediately. He ate the berries and nuts left there for him and watched, clinging to the vague hope that Nodak might still return. Not until the sun had passed overhead and the time for the midday meal had come and gone did he finally give up his lonely vigil.

Descending to the cave once more, he put on his high boots in preparation for the journey ahead. His weapons still lay on the rough wooden table in the corner of the cave. He looked at them hesitantly. What was it Nodak had said? That if he carried them he would become as bad as the Mollag. That possibility made him pause. And yet was it necessarily true? Why should he take the word of a man who had proved himself a thief? Also, there was the question of defence: surely he had the right to defend himself against those who hunted him. For a full minute he hesitated over what course to follow. In his heart he knew that his light weapons offered very little protection against the heavily armed Mollag. But he was frightened of again entering the forest alone; he wanted the reassuring feel of the bow across his back, the weight of the sword against his thigh. And at last, although he had the uneasy feeling of making a wrong choice, he armed himself as before and left the cave.

The forest was warm and still, only the highest branches moving in the light afternoon breeze. Here, there was very little undergrowth: the earth between the trees was covered with fine green moss; and the trees themselves, evenly spaced, rose sheer for over a hundred feet before putting out their first branches. Once he had left the hill behind, Quen felt as though he were moving through a huge airy building supported by the tall pillars of the trees and roofed over with a fine green lace of leaves which cast speckled patterns on the ground at his feet.

He was wary to begin with, creeping quietly from tree to tree, pausing frequently to glance furtively around him. But it soon became apparent that there were no Mollag in that part of Thual; that for the time at least he had shaken off his pursuers. It seemed that the only creatures who shared the forest with him were the tiny fan-tailed birds which came swooping down from the high branches to look at him, and the prick-eared squirrels which clung effortlessly to the tall smooth trunks. Sometimes large blue dragonflies zig-zagged between the shadows, stopping suddenly and hovering motionless in the warm shafts of sunlight.

Quen was still weak from his fever and for several days he wandered on slowly, resting whenever he felt the need, always working steadily towards the east – not because he knew that was the right direction, but because that was how he had started and it somehow seemed natural to travel towards the rising sun. For food, he picked the mushrooms which came bursting through the moss in the early morning, or gathered the nuts which fell from the high overhead branches. Occasionally he came across small red berries, sweet to the taste, which grew on vines coiling around the trunks of trees. At night he slept on the soft mossy ground. And for water he drank from the musty pools of dew and rain which gathered in the rocky hollows.

During those days of wandering, he felt happy and at peace, content merely to build up his strength.

Towards the end of the third day the forest began to change slightly: the trees became lower and thicker; and the clear ground gradually gave way to a tangle of undergrowth. He slept as usual in the open; but that night there was a heavy dew and he awoke cold, stiff, and hungry. To get warm, he ran swiftly along the twisting pathways until his face and limbs were glowing. Then, as on every other morning, he set about gathering the berries and nuts and mushrooms which had become his regular diet. Yet on this particular morning, although they took the edge off his appetite, they didn't seem to satisfy it. As he walked on he couldn't help thinking of the wheat cakes which his mother cooked on the open fire – and even more appetizing, of the meat and fish which his father occasionally brought home.

It was in this frame of mind that he came around a sharp bend in the path and suddenly found himself at the edge of a wide clearing. On the far side two deer were peacefully grazing in the shadow of some bushes. Without stopping to think, Quen reached up and drew the bow from his back. But even that slight movement had attracted the attention of the deer: they raised their broad wet muzzles and turned their heads slowly, scenting the breeze; then with a turn and a flick of their tails, they were gone.

Quen walked on, muttering angrily to himself. And now, whenever he detected a clearing ahead, he crouched down and approached it as silently as possible.

Towards noon, he again caught sight of a deer: a young buck with short, blunt, newly sprouting horns. It was grazing in a slight hollow about a hundred yards to the left of the path. Quen unslung his bow and reached for his quiver; but it was too long a shot for his light arrows. Dropping down onto his hands and knees, he began to crawl slowly around the edge of the hollow with the idea of coming up behind the deer. As he crawled, the tiny fan-tailed birds which had been his companions for days swooped down towards him, but he flicked at them angrily with his hands. All his attention was fixed on the deer, so that when he came to a young vine laden with sweet red berries, he trampled over it without even glancing down, crushing the ripe fruit underfoot.

At last he reached the far side of the hollow and carefully parted the bushes. The deer was slightly below him, its rich brown coat shining in the sunlight. It had moved away a little, but was still within bowshot. Fitting an arrow to his bow, Quen took careful aim at a spot immediately over the animal's heart.

The deer, as if sensing that something was wrong, raised its head and moved restlessly. Quen waited, steadying the bow, and then released the string with a twang. But at the very last moment the deer again stirred uneasily, and the arrow, instead of finding its heart, lodged in the joint of its shoulder.

With a snort, it turned, putting its weight on its wounded shoulder, and immediately fell. But it was up in an instant and running unsteadily across the hollow and into the trees. Quen slid down the shallow bank and followed it as fast as he could. Bushes ans branches whipped across his face as he ran dodging between the trees, but he hardly noticed them. He had forgotten the Mollag, his journey, everything, in his desire to catch the deer.

Within a few hundred yards he saw it standing, head lowered, knee-deep in forest ferns. The broken shaft of the arrow was still lodged in its shoulder and a stream of blood had stained its leg crimson. Remembering what the men of the village said (how a frightened animal will bleed faster and therefore tire and drop more quickly), Quen shouted and waved his arms, and the startled deer again bounded off through the trees. But it was easy enough to follow: every ten or fifteen paces, tell-tale drops of blood gleamed from the grass or bushes. Frequently, Quen caught glimpses of the deer at the turnings of paths; and each time that it whirled and lunged away it looked weaker. Once it staggered sideways and almost fell.

Quen, too, was tired by now; but he didn't slacken his pace. He believed that if he could keep the animal running it must soon drop. And he was right, because he came up to it soon afterwards in a narrow glade of tall grass closed in on all sides by thickly leaved trees. The deer had sagged forward onto its knees, but when it saw him it summoned the remainder of its strength, lowered its head, and backed away. Quen paused for a moment to catch his breath. Then he fitted another arrow to the bow and took careful aim.

But as he was about to shoot, there was a deafening roar from the side of the glade. The unexpected sound startled him so much that, in the act of releasing the string, he jerked his arm and the arrow flew harmlessly into the trees, missing the deer by a yard or more. Turning swiftly, Quen was confronted by a huge black bear which had moved quietly across the glade towards him. Frantically, he groped for another arrow, but the bear was almost upon him; and as he scurried backwards, he tripped in the tall grass, fell, and dropped his bow. There was no time to retrieve it. The bear roared again, directly above him, and he rolled sideways, regained his feet, and bolted into the trees.

Yet even as he ran, he knew that it was useless: no man on foot could match the speed of a bear's charge. He could hear the heavy body crashing through the forest behind him and he expected at every moment to feel the weight of the great paw upon his back. But the seconds passed and nothing happened. He continued to scramble blindly through the forest, dodging and twisting between the trees; and the bear followed just a few feet behind, grunting and growling as it pursued him. Quen thought, this is impossible – it was like some cruel dream or nightmare that must soon end. And yet the chase continued, with Quen struggling to maintain his speed even though he was close to exhaustion.

He had already been tired when he had reached the fallen deer: now, running for his life to escape the rush of the bear, he was soon gasping for breath, straining to draw more air into his aching lungs. More than once he nearly fell and only just managed to regain his balance. He had ceased to think or even to feel consciously afraid. He simply ran on, the bear still close behind, the trees and bushes flashing past in a green blur. He was so tired that he could no longer see clearly. In front of him the forest wavered – he tripped and stumbled and all at once his knees gave way, sending him sliding and rolling through the ferns. Something heavy and black leaped over him, and then, except for the noisy pounding of his own heart, there was silence.

He waited, lying face downwards in the ferns. Just for a few moments he was too exhausted to care what happened to him. But the silence continued and still he was lying there uninjured. Slowly, he raised his head and looked around. The bear was about fifteen feet away, watching him with its small dark eyes, its muzzle streaked with froth. Instead of charging once again, it merely growled a warning, tearing at the ground with one long-clawed paw.

Cautiously, Quen rose to his knees, his whole body sweating with fear. He knew that his short sword would be useless against the bear and that his only hope of survival was to work his way back to the glade, to where he had dropped his bow. But as soon as he began to crawl in that direction, the bear growled again and lumbered round to cut him off – though still it didn't attack, content merely to watch its victim.

Quen remained where he was for a minute or two, until the bear had settled onto all fours, and then began to crawl away once more, though in the opposite direction from the glade. This time the bear didn't try to prevent him. A soft growl issued from its throat and, with its thick blue tongue lolling from its mouth, it stood up and slowly began to follow.

After a short distance it became clear that the bear didn't intend to charge again, and Quen rose carefully to his feet. He walked slowly to begin with, gradually increasing his pace to a run, and still the bear remained about fifteen feet behind him. Only when he tried once again to work his way back to the glade did the great animal growl threateningly and cut across his path.

After that Quen gave up all thought of turning back. With no immediate possibility of escape, he ran or walked on, casting occasional nervous glances over his shoulder. Twice the bear growled loudly and moved up close on one side of him, forcing him to change direction slightly. But apart from those two incidents nothing happened to interrupt their silent passage through the forest.

Quen realized that he was being steered in a certain direction, much as a dog might herd a flock of sheep. And there was nothing he could do about it. He did think of trying to climb a tree and then of keeping the bear at bay with his sword. But only a moment's reflection was needed to reveal the foolishness of that scheme. He would almost certainly be forced down before he was more than a few feet from the ground; and in any case, the bear was probably a better tree-climber than he.

At the end of half an hour, all such schemes became unnecessary. Quen was following a half-overgrown path which opened abruptly into a clearing. Near the edge of the clearing the bear stopped and squatted on its haunches. Quen also stopped and looked back; but for some reason the bear seemed totally uninterested in him. Twisting its head around and down, it began to nuzzle and lick the shiny fur on its side. Encouraged by this sudden show of unconcern, Quen took one nervous step forward, and then another and another, until he had more than doubled the distance between him and the great beast.

He was almost in the middle of the clearing by then. On the far side was a line of thick bushes: if he could reach those and slip unseen back into the forest, he might yet stand a chance of escape. Taking care not to attract the bear's attention, he continued to walk softly away – when all at once, unexpectedly, the ground beneath his feet trembled and shook. Too late, he realized the trap into which he had walked, and he turned and tried to scramble clear. But as he did so, the bear roared and made as if to charge towards him. Instinctively he stopped and backed away. The ground shook again and gave way. He reached out in a futile attempt to save himself, his hands grasping at the empty air; and then he was falling down and down – not this time into unconsciousness, but into a deep pit sunk into the earth beneath his feet.

7 · The Servant

THE FALL knocked all the wind out of him and he lay for some time amongst the tangle of dry twigs and grass that had fallen with him. When at last he stood up he found he was in a deep straight-sided pit – so deep that all he could see above him was a fringe of grass and a clear circle of blue sky. His first thought was that he had fallen into a trap set by the Mollag; but then the bear's head appeared over the pit's edge, peering down at him, and he realized that the Mollag could not possibly have anything to do with this. They had no control over the beasts of the forest. Besides, he had not seen any of the grey armoured shapes for days. Obviously for the time being they had lost his trail. But if not the Mollag, who else could have set such a trap? And why?

He puzzled fruitlessly over these questions while the bear walked slowly around the pit, growling down at him, like some sentry put there to stand guard.

All the time the bear remained above, Quen knew there was no chance of escape and he sat down and waited, controlling his impatience and bewilderment as best he could. To his surprise, the bear did not remain for long: it patrolled the top of the pit several times, as though making sure that Quen was safely captured; and soon afterwards it ambled away into the forest.

Quen listened to it forcing its way through the bushes at the edge of the clearing and to the sound of its low growl growing fainter.

Left completely alone, Quen concentrated all his attention on the problem of escape. The pit was steep-sided, but the earth walls were rough and uneven, with large stones showing here and there. Resting his foot on one of these stones, he reached upwards, groping for handholds, and slowly began to climb. But when he had risen only a few feet, the soft earth crumbled and gave way and he slithered down to where he had started. He made the same attempt on other parts of the wall and always met with the same lack of success: the earth either broke in his hands or the stones dislodged beneath his feet.

Yet he was not to be beaten so easily. His next plan involved the mangled platform of sticks and grass which had fallen into the pit with him. Breaking these sticks into short lengths, he thrust them into the walls for hand- and footholds. But they were too dry and rotten, and as soon as he put his weight on them they snapped off and sent him sprawling backwards into the dirt.

After that he sat down for some time and thought. There was no way of making a ladder strong enough to take his weight, and although he could twist the dry grass into a makeshift rope, it would take too long; and even after it was finished there would be nothing to loop it over. Which meant that his only means of possible escape was the wall. But how? He leaned forward, resting his arms on his thighs as he puzzled over the problem, his elbow brushing against his scabbard. And immediately he had another idea.

Taking out his sword, he began cutting deep steps into the wall. The bottom of these he lined with small stones. When the first two were complete he carefully put his feet into them and tested them with his weight. This time they held. Without getting down, he cut other holes on the levels of his waist and head, picking the stones out of the earth all around him to strengthen the areas where his weight fell. In this way he slowly climbed up the wall, holding on with one hand and using the other to fashion more steps.

It was exhausting work and more than once he had to clamber down and rest. But slowly he went higher and higher, until finally he was able to hook one hand over the top edge of the pit. Sliding his sword back into its sheath, he put both hands over the edge and prepared to pull himself to safety. As he did so there was a faint sound from above. He hardly noticed it, concentrating on what had to be done. But in the act of straining upwards, he was suddenly confronted by a large hairy face only a foot or two from his own.

He was so startled that he very nearly fell. He released his hold, wavered backwards, and would have crashed down into the pit once more if two large hands had not reached down and saved him. He felt himself grabbed by the hair and the sleeve, and in an instant he was hauled up into the clearing and pushed roughly away from the gaping pit.

For a moment he lost his bearings. He steadied himself and noticed the bear sitting calmly in the grass. Then, for the first time, he saw his rescuer clearly: a muscular, heavily built man, covered from head to foot with fine brown hair. He was so hairy that he might almost have been taken for some strange beast if it had not been for his face and hands which were unmistakably human.

The man's appearance came as such a shock that Quen didn't even think of trying to run – though the man's swift movements soon made it clear that he would not have gone far. Leaping quickly forward, the man caught him by the shoulder, whirled him around, and plucked the remaining arrows from his quiver. While Quen watched, he frowned darkly to show his disapproval, and then snapped the arrows in two and flung the pieces away. The whole action was a kind of mime which expressed his dislike for such cruel and dangerous things far more clearly than words ever could have done. Yet he was not a mute: as Quen was to discover, he merely disliked using language unless it was absolutely necessary.

Now, pointing to his hairy body, he pronounced his own name:

'Namu.'

And having identified himself, he motioned with one hand, indicating that Quen should go before him, back into the forest. As if to support these signs, the bear came forward and pushed at

Quen with its muzzle, forcing him in a particular direction. Unable to refuse, Quen led the way, though to begin with he was not sure what was expected of him. Only gradually, after the bear had redirected him more than once, did he realize that he was being marched back to the glade where the wounded deer had made its stand.

It was mid-afternoon when they reached the glade and the deer was still there, lying in the long grass, its large eyes glazed with pain. The moment it saw Quen, it began struggling to its feet; but then it noticed Namu and sank back. It appeared completely untroubled by the presence of the bear.

As before, Namu said nothing, preferring actions to words. First he picked up the fallen bow, frowned at Quen, pointed to the deer, and immediately snapped the bow across his thick hairy knee. Next he went to the edge of the glade and began breaking thin lower branches from the trees. Although he had no idea what they were for, Quen drew his sword and helped, lopping the branches off cleanly with single strokes. Namu glanced over at the sword and frowned again, his hairy brows drawn together with disapproval, but he didn't take it away. When there was a small heap of sticks, he tied several of them together with twists of grass, to make a frame, and wove the others into the frame to form a crude kind of litter.

The deer, meanwhile, had not moved. It lay still, its shoulder caked with dry blood over which the tiny black forest flies swarmed. Now Namu knelt beside the wounded beast and pointed to the arrow, a questioning expression on his broad face.

'The point?' he asked quietly.

Quen understood what he meant: he wished to know what type of head the arrow carried, whether barbed or straight. If barbed, as in fact it was, then the arrow could not be pulled out, but must be cut free of the surrounding flesh.

At the thought of what had now to be done, Quen experienced a sudden overwhelming sense of shame. He wanted to tell this strange giant of a man that he had not intended to do this at all, that he had merely been hungry and had acted thoughtlessly. But in the presence of his silent companion he could not find the right words; and instead of speaking, he reached down, took the thin-bladed knife from his boot, and handed it to Namu.

'The arrow is barbed,' he murmured, and as he made the admission he blushed red with shame.

He expected Namu to react angrily, but instead the big man only shook his head in sorrow; and watching him, Quen saw with amazement that there was no room in those deep brown eyes for such emotions as hatred and anger. Despite his size and his savage, hairy appearance, there was a gentleness about him which Quen had never encountered before.

With one swift movement Namu cut deep into the wound and lifted the arrow clear. The simple operation was over so quickly that the deer barely realized what had happened. It strained forward nervously, and Namu comforted it with one hand, while with the other he took a thick wad of dried moss from the woollen pouch which hung at his shoulder. Clamping the moss on the freshly bleeding wound, he tied it securely in place with twists of grass. This done, he lifted the heavy animal effortlessly onto the litter, motioning Quen to lift one corner; and together they dragged the litter out of the glade and along a broad, well-used path which led to the north.

For a time, Quen bore up his corner of the litter without too much difficulty. But the load was heavy, and slowly the strain began to tell on him. Eventually he reached the point where he could go no further.

'Can't we rest?' he gasped out. 'Just for a while?'

It was as if he had not spoken: Namu, without so much as turning his head, continued forward; and when Quen, his arms aching, tried to slacken his pace, the bear moved up and nudged him from behind.

From that point on the journey was a difficult and painful one. Through his growing weariness, Quen realized that this, like his earlier frantic flight from the bear, was part of some general punishment for what he had done. Where that punishment would lead him and how it would end, he had no idea. Nor did he seem to have any choice in the matter. Like a slave, he trudged on, his arms feeling as though they were being wrenched from their sockets. Even when he stumbled and fell he was not permitted to rest: Namu lifted him gently yet firmly to his feet, placed the corner of the litter back in his hands, and pressed on.

Quen remembered the final stage of the journey as in a vague dream. There seemed to be endless shady miles of twisting pathway, and then he was stumbling out of the forest into the open sunlight. The litter was taken from his numb hands and for a long time he lay face downwards in cool green grass.

When, finally, he had recovered his strength, it was late afternoon and long shadows were streaking the grass. Sitting up, he found himself in a large open area roughly the shape of a diamond. In the centre of the diamond was the strangest house he had ever seen. It was not built of earth or hewn wood or stone, like other dwellings, but of living trees. Two rows of young fir trees had been bent towards each other and their tops tied together to form a rough arch or tent shape. More trees had been planted at each end, while vines and creepers grew thickly over the whole living structure, making it snug and waterproof.

This unusual house was not the only strange thing about the open space. Wherever he looked, Quen saw animals of many different types: rabbits and deer grazing peacefully; foxes and badgers blinking sleepily in the late afternoon light; brown and black bears ambling across the grass; hares sitting up, watchful and alert or bounding between the trees; a small pack of wolves eyeing the other animals narrowly, but remaining quiet and docile, as though this diamond-shaped space were a magic circle within which no harm could befall any living creature. There were also hundreds of birds: shy robins and wrens; squawking magpies and crows; swifts and swallows skimming inches above the grass and then sweeping up into the sky; hawks, ravens, owls, and many more; with one huge golden eagle sitting calm and serene on the topmost branch of the tree house.

Quen stood up, amazed by what he saw, and went over to the house. Namu was waiting there, the deer still lying on the litter beside him, its eyes half-closed in pain and sickness. Taking another wad of moss from his pouch, Namu handed it to Quen and pointed to the animal's wounded shoulder. Quen understood what was wanted, and kneeling down he carefully replaced the dressing. When he had finished, Namu nodded, and pressing one hairy finger on Quen's chest, pronounced a single word:

46

'Servant.'

'I am the servant?' Quen asked uncertainly.

Again the huge man nodded.

'Must I remain here and be your servant?'

This time Namu shook his head.

'Servant,' he said again, and taking Quen gently by the shoulder, he pointed first to the wounded deer and then to all the other animals within the open space. After that, without another word, he turned and disappeared into the tree house.

There could be no doubt what he meant. This, Quen realized, was to be his punishment: to act as a humble servant to the animals of the forest. Too late, he remembered Nodak's warning – how the man who carries weapons will always be tempted to use them. Now, it seemed, he must pay the price. And with little chance of escape, for the great bear which had followed him since midday still crouched watchfully nearby.

The evening shadows were beginning to lengthen. Quen looked longingly towards the forest. He had a sudden desire to run away, to continue his journey. Yet he knew that was impossible. His journey had ended here; he would never reach the Wise Ones, nor bring help to his family and the people of the ten villages. How badly he had failed! And with a cry of regret, he sank miserably down onto the grass.

8 · The Lesson Learned

QUEN made his only attempt at escape that first night. Namu had gone into the house some time before and the whole clearing was quiet – even the bear had walked off into the darkness. Rising stealthily from the grass where he had been left to sleep, Quen made his way softly towards the forest which showed as a dark line against the starlit sky. But he didn't get very far: before he had gone twenty paces, an owl began hooting from the trees and within seconds he was surrounded by the wolves. They did not attack him, but their eyes glowed in the darkness and they snarled and snapped if he made the slightest movement; so that it was a relief when the bear ambled into the circle and nudged him back to where he was supposed to be sleeping.

Namu made no reference to this incident the following morning. At dawn he emerged from the tree house and immediately pointed to the wounded deer, making it plain that the animal was Quen's responsibility. Once the animal had been seen to, its wound cleaned and dressed, Namu gave Quen the first of the many tasks which were to occupy him throughout the light hours.

In the days that followed, Quen did many jobs, accompanied wherever he went by the bear. He chopped hay in the forest glades, carrying great piles of it back to the house on the litter; he gathered pouchfuls of nuts and berries which he dried in the sun and stored away for the winter; he cleaned the coats of the animals, picking ticks from between the spines of the hedgehogs or from the large ears of fox and deer; and when necessary he helped Namu to doctor sick and wounded creatures, setting broken limbs or mending the delicate flight feathers of the birds.

Although the work was rarely heavy, there was a great deal of it and he was usually busy from dawn till sunset. Yet oddly enough he never really resented it. This was largely because from the outset he took a special interest in the wounded deer. Every possible moment was spent tending or watching over it; he even slept close to it at night in case he was needed. More than once he wondered how he could have brought himself to shoot at the poor creature, especially as the forest, its soil and trees and vines, had provided him with all the food he required; and he knew, without needing to be told, that if the deer were to die, the guilt would be his alone. On the other hand, it was not simply his guilt which concerned him: more than anything else it was the deer itself that he came to care for.

For the first three days it remained on the brink of death, its eyes closed, its head drooping or resting on the ground. The wound swelled dangerously and nothing Quen did seemed to make any difference. He cleaned it regularly and applied the herbs which Namu gave him, but all without success. The swelling continued despite his efforts. He had almost given up hope when, on the morning of the fourth day, he awoke and found the animal revived, its head raised, looking at him. Also, and what pleased him almost as much, it showed no fear or nervousness when he approached.

That was a day of great excitement: the wound showed definite signs of healing and in the afternoon the deer actually took food from his hand. From then on it recovered rapidly and at the end of a week was on its feet once more and hobbling around the tree house. For Quen it meant more than success: it was as though a great weight had been lifted from his heart; he felt that he had never been quite so relieved and happy before and for the moment he forgot about his ruined journey and the Mollag who pursued him.

Yet he was not allowed to forget for very long: one morning, as he was returning through the forest with a pouchful of berries, the bear suddenly stopped beside him and growled, the thick fur rising on the back of its neck. Sensing danger, Quen also stopped and peered through the undergrowth. Nothing stirred and he would probably have walked on had the bear not reared up and pawed angrily at the air, while at the same time letting out one of its terrible roars. Quen looked up and there, on an overhanging branch high above the path, only dimly visible through the leaves, was the face of a Mollag soldier: the dead grey skin, the round sunken eyes and exposed nostrils, the twin horns curving across the low forehead.

With a cry of alarm, Quen bolted down the path, the bear following close behind. He didn't stop until he reached the tree house where, panting for breath, he told Namu briefly of the Mollag and of the danger they were in. Obviously Namu himself had already encountered the Mollag in the forest because he took the warning seriously. Without hesitation, he entered the house and gathered up the few necessary things he wished to take with him.

Yet even that slight delay proved perilous: as he emerged from the house, there was a series of jagged shouts from the forest and a line of Mollag soldiers came charging out onto the open ground. They were armed not with sword or spear, as was normal, but with wooden clubs; and even in that split second before he turned to flee, it crossed Quen's mind that a club was the kind of weapon used not for killing a man, but for taking him alive.

With characteristic speed, Namu let out a shrill cry and instantly all the animals and birds made for the safety of the forest. Then, scooping Quen up under one arm, he also ran swiftly towards the distant trees.

Pressed lightly against the thick furry body, Quen felt peculiarly safe, despite his fear of the Mollag. For some reason he had total faith in Namu's ability to outwit and even to outrun their pursuers. Also, there was the bear which he could hear pounding along behind them. With such swift and strong allies, he was confident of escaping the Mollag as he had before.

Yet to his surprise, when they were only a short way into the forest Namu stopped.

'The Mollag are close . . .' Quen began urgently, and quickly Namu pressed a hairy palm over his mouth, stifling the words.

Before he could argue, Namu took him in both hands and lifted him high into the air, close to the branch of a nearby tree. Realizing what was expected of him, Quen grasped the branch and scrambled up in amongst the twigs and leaves. From there he was completely hidden from the ground. Pulling aside a layer of leaves he looked down: Namu and the bear were directly below him. In a sudden and unexpected show of friendship, the huge wild-looking man raised his hand and touched the bough on which Quen stood.

'Stay,' he said softly, and for the very first time he smiled so that Quen, without having to be told in words, knew that the past was forgiven. There was no time to return the smile, for like the flickering of a shadow across the ground, both Namu and the bear were gone.

The Mollag soldiers followed soon afterwards. Crouched in amongst the leaves, Quen heard their heavy, regular tread pass beneath him and gradually disappear into the forest. He parted the leaves once again, slowly, taking care to make no sound, and peered out. Nothing moved and there were no signs of Mollag sentries. The soldiers had seen him being picked up and carried off, and now they were following Namu's tracks, believing that he, Quen, was still ahead of them. That meant that he could almost certainly climb down and continue his interrupted journey. Yet Namu had told him to stay there and so for the time he didn't move.

Midday came, the afternoon wore slowly away, and still he didn't move. Not until the sun was low in the sky was he startled into action – not by anything around him, but by a sudden disturbing thought. He remembered how all the animals had run for safety at the sound of Namu's urgent cry. But what of his wounded deer whose damaged shoulder made it impossible for it to run or even walk any distance?

With mingled feelings of fear and dread, Quen swung down from the branch and ran back to the tree house. Nothing stirred

51

in the large diamond-shaped clearing, but over on the far side he could see a brown shape in the grass. He hurried over, knowing already what he would find. The deer was lying still and dead, killed by the Mollag, its body already stiff and cold. There was no sense in the killing: they had taken no part of the body for food; they had simply struck it down as it hobbled towards the forest.

Yet as he stared at the still body, Quen was not thinking of the Mollag themselves. All he could recall clearly were Nodak's words, the warning given to him in the hidden cave: 'If you choose to carry weapons, you become no better than the Mollag.' No better than the Mollag! The simple truth of those words struck him now with painful force. He thought bitterly: I am the one to blame; nobody else. If it weren't for me this poor creature would still be running free somewhere within Thual. And he burst into tears, not only of grief, but also of rage at his own folly. Taking his sword from its sheath, he ran over to a large pointed rock which rose out of the ground and struck the blade against it until it shivered into a dozen pieces.

In the brief silence which followed, there was a faint stirring in the nearby bushes. He whirled around, still caught up in his rage, determined to stand and fight whatever the cost. But nobody was there – only the evening breeze rustling the leaves and branches. And as his anger cooled, it occurred to him that his determination to fight, to kill or be killed, was precisely what Nodak had warned him against: it was what had led to this senseless killing here before him.

Calmer now, he took out his small knife and weighed it thoughtfully in his hand. Should this also be destroyed? He hesitated and finally put it back into the side of his boot, vowing to himself that he would keep it only as a simple tool.

Already it was almost dusk. With the broken stump of the sword, he began the painful task of digging a shallow grave. It took him some time, and when he replaced the last sod it was completely dark. While he worked, he had felt more than once that he was not alone and he knew that his safest course was to hide in the forest. But he was unwilling to leave the grave so soon. He therefore dismissed his fears and sat down in the grass to wait and watch the night through. That was what his people in the village always did if someone died, and it seemed only right that he should observe this practice now.

He had not meant to close his eyes, but as the night advanced his head gradually sank forward and he fell into a light sleep. He was awoken from it suddenly by a heavy crashing in the undergrowth behind him. Springing to his feet, he ran to one side and slipped quickly into the cover of the forest. From there he listened and watched. Nothing happened for a moment or two: then a dark figure crept out of the trees, moved silently over to the grave mound, and immediately crept back into the shadows.

Quen gave whoever it was plenty of time to leave the area before he too came cautiously out of hiding. What the unknown visitor had wanted he had no idea. But when he was close to the grave he noticed something on top of it. He bent down and instantly recognized the small cloth bag which Faya had given to him. Quickly pulling it open, he upended it over his cupped hand. By then a half moon had risen and was shining pale and clear over Thual. In its feeble light he saw in the palm of his hand, rose-shaped and glistening, his lost diamond. His stone, his sign, returned to him at last.

9 · The Journey Continued

To QUEN'S relieved eyes, the diamond had never appeared quite so brilliant, like a glittering point of light in the darkness. Just having it in his possession once again made him feel more confident and hopeful, the future less gloomy and threatening; and for the rest of the night he remained watchful and alert beside the freshly dug grave.

Shortly before dawn, his vigil over, he went to the tree house to collect some of the dried nuts and berries to take with him on his journey. As he was scooping them into a woollen pouch left there by Namu, he was startled by a rustling noise near the entrance. He turned and caught a glimpse of a small animal creeping into the house. Even in the poor light he could see that it was a fox, its eyes gleaming, ears pricked forward, large bushy tail almost touching the ground. It seemed natural enough that the animal should come there at such a time, and Quen took little notice of it. He knew that foxes, like many of the other nocturnal creatures, looked upon the house as a place of peace and refuge during the daylight hours.

Yet to Quen's surprise, when he set out at first light the fox did not remain behind. Instead, it bounded nervously across the open grass and waited for him in the shelter of the trees. Puzzled, Quen tried to shoo it away.

'Get back to the house,' he said, waving his arms.

But the animal merely backed off and waited, nostrils quivering, its eyes never still, shifting watchfully from side to side. Something about its appearance reminded Quen of the past, of words spoken to him some time before. He hunted back through his memory and recalled his mother's advice on the morning before his departure. Arguing with Lod, she had said of Quen: 'He will have to rely on his cunning.' Yes, that was it, his cunning – far more useful to him than the short sword he had smashed against the rock. And what could be more cunning than the fox, an animal renowned for its ability to outwit man?

Readjusting the strap of the pouch across his chest, Quen smiled at the small watchful creature.

'Perhaps you will bring me luck on the journey,' he said, and he set off once more towards the east.

For the first few minutes the fox followed behind, but only until it was sure of the intended direction: then it slipped past Quen and led the way. Quen didn't try to stop it: he had begun to suspect that the animal was perhaps sent by Namu, in which case he would do well to keep close to it. Also, he had grown strangely used to the companionship of the bear and was glad not to be alone. So, fixing his eyes on the reddish brush bobbing in front of him, he settled into a steady jogging run, a pace which he could maintain for most of the day. His plan at that stage was simply to cover as many miles as possible.

The fox, however, had other ideas. Before they had gone very far it stopped, backtracked for some distance to a patch of rocky ground, and then leaped into the undergrowth. From the outset, Quen was aware of what was happening: he had heard of the ways of the fox and he could see that this small creature was intent on confusing any possible pursuers. Treading carefully within his former tracks, Quen followed the fox into the undergrowth. Together they travelled back in a wide circle, joining the path close to the clearing. Again they set out to the east, and again the fox took to the undergrowth, this time striking across country until they encountered a narrow little-used path to the north.

This process of circling and backtracking went on all morning and by midday they had covered only half the distance Quen had hoped for. On the other hand, they had left a confusing trial which it would take even a master woodsman hours to unravel.

By mid-afternoon, Quen was forced to rest: he was hot and tired, his arms and legs scratched and sore from pushing his way through bushes and tall ferns. The fox, its coat gleaming red and brown in the leaf-speckled sunlight, seemed as fresh as ever; yet as if sensing the boy's fatigue, it led him soon afterwards to a dark silent river, deep and slow-moving, bordered by great willows and bristling stands of poplar. Here Quen drank his fill and ate some of the food he carried before taking to the water and drifting downstream – the fox floating beside him, its brush riding high, its pointed snout thrust out ahead.

That restful period in the river refreshed him and he was able to continue their twisting elusive journey for several more hours. Nonetheless, by nightfall he was so exhausted that he barely had sufficient energy to crawl into the base of a hollow tree to which the fox had led him.

He awoke only once in the night, disturbed by the shrill cry of a dying rabbit. He called softly into the darkness, and when there was no answering sound, he guessed that what he had heard was the fox making its nightly kill. Vaguely, he wondered why it was that he should be punished for daring to hunt in the sacred forest, when creatures like the fox and weasel preyed continually on those weaker than themselves. But before he could think of an answer to the problem, he had drifted once more into a deep sleep.

The next two days followed exactly the pattern of the first, and Quen, who had begun by feeling grateful to the fox, grew steadily more impatient. The continual twisting and dodging, the crawling through thorny undergrowth, which had once seemed such an essential safety measure, now appeared both tiresome and unnecessary. Surely they had confused their pursuers by now. To the tired and bedraggled Quen, the endless backtracking and travelling in circles slowly became nothing more than a waste of time.

By the morning of the fourth day he had reached the limits of his patience. They had just spent nearly an hour forcing their way through some of the thickest forest growth Quen had yet encountered. And now, no sooner had they returned to the path than the fox suddenly stopped, sniffed at a patch of level leaf-strewn ground, and again took to the woods, its small sinuous body sliding off between the trees. Quen had had enough: his skin was scratched and torn and more than anything else he wanted to keep to the smooth pathway for a while. Ignoring the fox, he continued straight ahead, determined to pursue his own course for the rest of the day.

But within no more than three strides he realized his mistake and the reason for the fox's suspicion. With a swishing noise, the leafy ground all around seemed to curl up and enclose him; and before he could leap clear he was jerked upside down and hauled up into the trees as if by invisible hands. When he finally managed to right himself, he found he was swinging high above the ground, caught in a thick rope net. Obviously it had been spread across the path by the Mollag and sprinkled with leaves; and he, ignoring the fox's silent warning, had stepped right into it.

The immediate problem was how to get out. He reached up through the thick overhang of oak leaves, feeling for the neck of the net, and found that it was tightly closed by a wire draw-string. The wire had bitten deeply into the rope loops and there was nothing he could do to loosen them. Very well, he decided, he would have to cut his way out; and he pushed his fingers down the side of his boot, searching for the knife he kept there. But to his dismay it was gone. Frantically he felt in the other boot – that too was empty.

What could have happened to it? Only the previous evening he had used it to cut small branches for a bed; and he was sure he had replaced it in his boot afterwards. With an effort, he controlled his feeling of desperation and tried to think clearly. Either he had lost the knife somewhere in the forest, or (and this seemed more likely) it had dropped from his boot when he had been jerked upside down by the net – in which case it would be somewhere on the ground below. Peering down between his feet, he searched the pathway and immediately spotted the tip of the bone handle protruding from a small heap of leaves directly beneath him.

During the next two hours, Quen racked his brains for a means of escape, but without success. He had no way of cutting the ropes, which were too thick to bite through, or of loosening the draw-string. He tried pulling himself up into the tree above, but the sheer weight of the net, dragging down onto his shoulders, forced him to release his hold. He even tried unravelling the woollen pouch and using the wool thread as a kind of lasso with which to gather the knife below him; but the thread was too soft and pliable and as soon as he touched the bone handle it slipped deeper into the leaves. Reluctantly he gave up all hope of freeing himself: the only possible way out of the net was to wait for the Mollag who had originally set the trap. Inevitably, it seemed, he must be captured.

That was bad enough; yet, strangely, what worried Quen even more was the idea of his diamond falling into Mollag hands. He thought, rather wildly, of throwing it down to the fox which all the time had sat waiting on the ground below, its sharp pointed face looking sadly up at him. But then, what if the fox ignored it? No, the only thing to do was to hide it securely. Lifting the edge of his tunic, he loosened a tiny section of the hem and slipped the cloth bag through, working it along the inside of the hem until it was far from the small hole.

He had no sooner done this than the fox gave a low warning bark and slunk away out of sight. Moments later, Quen heard a familiar tread and a Mollag soldier came down the path and stopped beneath the tree. When he saw Quen he didn't smile or laugh. Like all the Mollag, he had only one means of showing pleasure, and that was to shout. Opening his mouth, he called out in a sharp metallic voice, a loud inhuman cry of triumph. Looking down, Quen saw the thick purplish tongue which almost filled the mouth, and above and below it the ridged yellowish bone which served as teeth.

He waited silently as the Mollag went to a nearby tree, reached up, and cut through the rope which held the net. There was a tearing of leaves above his head and he dropped to the earth, hitting the hard ground with a jarring thud. Yet winded and half-stunned as he was by the fall, he still had the presence of mind to grope furtively in the leaves all around him. He found what he wanted, the familiar bone handle, and while the Mollag was cutting him free of the net, he slipped the knife back into his boot.

For the second time in his life he steeled himself for the icy touch of those three-fingered hands. He knew he must be searched and it would be better at this stage not to resist. But in spite of his resolve, when the dead-grey hands reached down to grasp him, his nerve failed; and rolling clear he tried to dodge past the Mollag and leap away into the forest.

There was just a chance he might have succeeded had he been better prepared. But he was stiff from being curled up in the net and still slightly winded from the fall. Instead of springing past the guard as he intended, he made only a half-hearted staggering stride which failed to carry him clear. It was all the opportunity that the Mollag needed: raising his wooden club, he swung it directly at Quen. There was no time to duck or draw back: he put up one hand defensively and the full force of the blow fell straight across his forearm. He heard a sharp crack, a pain shot up his arm and into his shoulder, and even before he fell he knew with near certainty that his arm was broken.

In those first few minutes the pain was so great that he was hardly aware of being searched. He was dimly conscious of cold fingers running over his tunic and body, but that was all. Not until he was roughly pushed from behind and he found himself again moving off through the forest did he realize that both the stone and the knife had remained undiscovered. In his present desperate situation that now seemed a small victory; but it was the only glimmer of hope remaining to him, and through the swirling mist of pain he clung to it grimly.

10 · Captive

DESPITE his broken arm and the obvious pain he was in, Quen was not allowed to rest throughout the remainder of that day. The squat square-bodied Mollag lumbered along behind, prodding him between the shoulder blades with his club whenever Quen slackened his pace. Nursing his injured left arm with his other hand, he stumbled down the gloomy tree-covered trail for mile after mile, continually on the lookout for a chance of breaking free of his captor. But what little hope he still had seemed to vanish altogether when, late in the afternoon, they were joined by another Mollag – a huge evil-smelling figure dressed in greasy leather and scarred greenish-bronze plates. He let out a great roar when he saw Quen and cuffed him on the side of the head, knocking him down; but immediately the other Mollag restrained him, rasping out something in his own tongue, and together all three moved off once again, Quen travelling between them, half-choked by the corpse-like smell of the two grey-skinned soldiers.

The Mollag themselves would not normally have stopped to rest, but soon after nightfall Quen was so obviously tired out that it was a question of either carrying him or allowing him to sleep. They debated the matter in their clipped metallic speech and finally threw him down beneath a tree and lit a small fire of leaves and twigs. Each of them carried a light pack on his back, and from these they took stringy pieces of raw sour-smelling meat which they singed on the fire and wolfed down. One of them tossed a piece to Quen, but he kicked it away with his foot, refusing even to touch it.

'As hunger grows inside you,' the Mollag said, 'you will learn to act differently. In a day or two you will beg us for the scraps that fall from our fingers.'

'A day or two?' Quen asked sharply. 'Where are you taking me then?'

'To where you came from: back to the ten villages.'

The thought of retracing all those miles only to face his parents with nothing achieved was almost more than he could bear at that moment, tired and dispirited as he was.

'But why there?' he cried. 'Why not ask me what you want now? Do what you have to do here and be done with it.'

'Be silent!' the Mollag ordered. 'It is not for us to question you. You are to be taken before Ungeth. That is his command.'

Quen had heard vague rumours of there being a Mollag leader; yet nobody had been sure that such a figure actually existed.

'Who is Ungeth?' he asked. 'Is he your king?'

'King!' the Mollag said disdainfully. 'He cannot be described by such stupid words. He is Ungeth, the supreme one. Now be quiet and sleep. There will be no more talk until we bring you before him.'

The Mollag came over to where Quen lay and tied his hands and legs together with leather thongs. Quen did not resist. For some reason which he did not fully understand, the knowledge that the Mollag were subject to a supreme leader cheered him slightly. Somehow it gave him the feeling that he was not up against a whole army, but simply one figure – Ungeth. His dying hopes suddenly flickered alive again: perhaps, after all, there was a weakness at the very heart of the vast Mollag strength.

Although Quen was tired, he struggled to stay awake. Now, more than ever, he felt the need to regain his freedom. Through half-closed eyes he watched the two Mollag muttering beside the fire. Beyond them the forest formed a single black curtain which the tiny fire could not penetrate. Quen was gazing longingly at the promised safety of this darkness when abruptly his attention was caught by a flash of moving light. He blinked to bring himself fully awake and found himself staring at a pair of watchful eyes.

. Almost at the same instant the Mollag also noticed the eyes and leaped to their feet; but before they could so much as draw their clubs, a terrible chorus of howls broke out and more than a dozen pairs of eyes appeared in the darkness all around them. Like the Mollag, Quen recognized those howls immediately: they were the cries of a wolf pack which was only yards away, preparing to attack. Quen's first reaction was one of fear. But as the Mollag scrabbled in the fire, searching for brands large enough to fling into the darkness, he realized how foolish he was being. Here, at last, was the opportunity he had hardly dared to hope for.

Ignoring the pain in his broken arm, he arched his back and reached down to his boot, to where the knife was hidden. With the bone handle grasped firmly in his good hand, he sliced through the leather thongs binding his feet. Then, while the Mollag were busy trying to scare off the wolf pack, he rolled over onto his knees and stumbled to his feet.

He had no idea what awaited him beyond the narrow ring of light. It could be a swift death from the savage jaws of the wolves. Yet at that moment even such a possibility seemed preferable to being held and ultimately tortured by the Mollag. And drawing a deep breath, he stepped into darkness.

Directly ahead of him two pairs of eyes glinted threateningly. But instead of coming closer, they narrowed and faded into the darkness on either side. He paused, giving himself a chance to grow used to the sudden darkness; and as he did so, something brushed against his leg. Reaching down with his still-bound hands, he touched a soft furry coat, and just for an instant he thought a wolf had sidled up to him; but then he caught the unmistakable musky smell of fox, and all at once he understood exactly what was happening. This was not really an attack at all, but more a kind of rescue. Somewhere in the forest Namu still protected him. And without any further hesitation he ran off between the trees.

Gradually the shouts of the Mollag and the howling of the wolves faded behind him. The fox had led him directly to a broad path, open to the sky; and now, by the faint light of the stars, he mustered the last of his strength, determined to put as great a distance between himself and the Mollag as possible. He knew they could not follow him at night and that provided he kept moving he could gain six or more hours on them before dawn. Then there would be time to rest. Meanwhile, his immediate task was to reach water and cover his tracks.

As on a previous occasion, the fox seemed to sense his needs, and before the night was half over it had led him to a shallow rocky stream. Here, he stopped for the first time to free his hands. Squatting down, he took the knife between his teeth and sawed through the leather thong. His wrists and fingers were stiff and numb from being bound so long, and it was while he sat, chafing his uninjured hand against his thigh to bring back the circulation, that he realized the full extent of his weariness. Fearful that he might either lose the will to go on or simply sink into an exhausted sleep, he clambered up and splashed off down the rocky bed of the stream.

During the last two hours of darkness, he was forced to slow down. Yet when the sky finally began to lighten he was still moving, though only at a slow unsteady walk. By then he was in desperate need of rest. He had had no sleep for twenty-four hours, and his broken arm jolted him with pain at every step. In addition, a light rain had begun to fall – not enough to cover his tracks, but sufficient to soak him through. Normally, that would not have affected him; but in his exhausted state he was soon chilled to the bone.

In the full light of the new day he looked a sorry sight. With his hair plastered to his forehead, his face pale and drawn, his eyes hollow with fatigue, and his damaged arm swollen and hanging uselessly at his side, he staggered to a halt just where the path divided into two. The fox was already scurrying off, urging him on, but he could go no further and he looked around, searching for a hollow log or tree – any place that was dry and warm, where he could curl up and rest.

The forest, however, had never appeared more unfriendly and forbidding. From a grey overcast sky the rain fell steadily, dripping from the leaves and bushes, streaking the trunks of trees with damp. It seemed impossible to imagine that the sun ever shone in such a dank gloomy place, and the task of finding a dry refuge seemed hopeless. With his teeth chattering uncontrollably, Quen gave up his search almost before it was begun. Staggering into the partial shelter of a large elm tree, he was about to sink down onto the open ground when he heard the fox give its soft warning bark and he turned to see it scurrying back towards him.

There was now no question of outrunning his pursuers: he had reached a stage where he lacked not only the energy, but also the will to go on. And creeping between the bushes, he climbed over a rotting, fallen log and lay down in the thick wet grass. The fox, after hesitating for a moment, followed him; and together they peered down the narrow track to where it bent away out of sight.

They didn't have long to wait. Through the mist of rain which seemed to hang in the air, Quen saw a flicker of movement and then two figures emerged into full view. To his relief they were not the Mollag. Instead, a man and a woman came walking down the path: both of them tall, with long pale faces, and dressed in full-length white robes and broad-brimmed white hats. Their hair too was long and had been drawn around their faces and tied under the chin. In the case of the man, hair and beard mingled together and covered most of his chest, reaching almost to his waist.

Both man and woman walked slowly, their bright observant eyes continually probing the forest. So as not to be seen, Quen ducked completely out of sight. Nonetheless, as they drew close to where he lay, they became steadily more suspicious, their eyes flashing uneasily from side to side. Finally, when they were directly opposite the fallen log, they stopped altogether.

'It is no use hiding,' the woman said. 'Come out and show yourself.'

At the sound of the low commanding voice, the fox leaped over the log and ran past the two figures as though trying to attract their attention; but they showed no interest in the small animal.

'I know you can hear me,' the woman said. 'I command you, in the sacred name of Thual, to show yourself.'

Quen had no desire to be taken again; common sense told him to remain out of sight and to try to creep further away. Yet somehow that was impossible. An invisible force seemed to envelop him, and almost against his will he found himself slowly rising to his feet and turning to face the fierce shining eyes of these tall unknown figures. As though from a great distance, he heard the man say:

'It is the boy, the one we have been searching for.'

And the woman's reply:

'He will have to answer for his presence here.'

11 · The Pale Keepers

ALTHOUGH he was powerless to move, Quen knew well enough what had happened to him: he had escaped from the Mollag only to fall into the hands of the Pale Keepers, the chief guardians of Thual. During his childhood he had heard too many stories about the tall white-robed figures not to recognize them now. As he stood facing them it even occurred to him that perhaps Namu and the fox had rescued him not merely out of friendship, but rather to lead him into precisely this trap. At that moment such a possibility did not disturb him unduly: in his exhausted condition his only immediate fear was that he would be forced to continue walking.

Fortunately, that fear at least was groundless. The woman, whose name he learned was Ildaron, perceived instantly that he was in no fit state to travel. She also noticed how his left arm hung heavy and limp at his side.

'Come here, boy,' she said sternly.

He stumbled towards her and stood swaying on the open path.

'What has happened to your arm?' she asked, not unkindly.

'It was broken by the Mollag,' he mumbled.

She exchanged knowing glances with her companion.

'This must be attended to right away,' she said.

Taking Quen by the shoulder, she led him into the partial shelter of the elm tree he had stopped under earlier. Totally unable to resist, Quen waited passively as she felt along the arm, delicately fingering the swollen area.

'I shall have to reset the bone,' she said quietly.

By way of answer, her tall companion measured roughly half-way along the wooden staff he was carrying and broke it in two across his knee. Next, he knelt behind Quen and held him firmly. Quen, meanwhile, was not sure what was being done to him. He watched as Ildaron took his arm in both hands – and then there was a flash of pain so sudden and so intense that it seemed to rise right up into his head and to engulf him. Before he could so much as cry out, he swayed drunkenly and fainted.

When he came to, the sharp pain had gone, leaving only a dull ache, and he was lying safe and warm in the hollow trunk of a tree. The tree itself, an oak, was still growing, and from where he lay he could look up through a narrow opening at the protective layer of leaves which clustered thickly above him. He tried to move his injured arm, but it was strapped across his body, the two pieces of wooden staff bound on either side of it to prevent any movement below the elbow. With his right arm he levered himself up and looked out: the rain had stopped and he could tell from the light that it was mid-afternoon. Mid-afternoon! That meant he had slept too long and had lost his valuable lead over the Mollag. Rising to his knees, he crawled through the narrow entrance and out into the open.

The woman was sitting at the foot of the tree, as though waiting for him.

'You have slept well,' she said.

'You should have woken me,' he answered. 'I was running from the Mollag: they will be close behind us by now.'

'If they are,' she said calmly, 'we shall soon find out, because Fraylon has gone back along your tracks to assess the danger. Fraylon is my companion – I am called Ildaron. You, I know, are Quen.'

'It is too dangerous to wait,' Quen said urgently. 'I tell you they are close behind. Every minute is important.'

She shook her head.

'We cannot leave until Fraylon returns.'

As if in response to her statement, there was a faint murmur as of wind gently rustling the leaves, and Fraylon came running between the trees.

'It is as we feared,' he said. 'The Mollag are less than an hour from here, following the boy's trail.'

Ildaron stood up, looking concerned for the first time.

'That is too close,' she said. 'In his condition the boy cannot keep ahead of them until nightfall. We could carry him between us, but that would leave a trail that might be followed even after dark.'

'True,' Fraylon said, nodding. 'That is why you and the boy must go on ahead. I can hold them long enough to give you a start.'

'That is the only way?' she asked.

He nodded again:

'There is no other.'

'But the Mollag will kill you,' Quen broke in. 'There are two of them.'

The long pale face, framed by hair and beard, turned towards him.

'I do not think they will succeed in harming me,' he said quietly. 'But even if they do, it will make no difference. Our duty is to take you to the Caverns and deliver you into the hands of Alron. Nothing must prevent that. Now make ready to leave.'

So saying, he reached into a slit in his white robe and pulled out what appeared to be a handful of moss and feathers. When this strange material was smoothed out, Quen saw that it was a kind of soft outer shoe. Fraylon produced another of these from his robe and fitted them both over the lower half of Quen's boots. Ildaron had also pulled some onto her feet.

'With these,' Fraylon explained, 'you will walk like the cat, and leave as little trace.'

Quen was not sure whether to thank him or not. He realized clearly enough that Fraylon was risking his life to save him from the Mollag. At the same time, he was still a captive, being saved only so that he could be taken to a distant place where, for all he knew, some punishment or other awaited him. Before he could make up his mind what to say, Fraylon had turned towards his companion. Reaching above his head, he placed the fingertips of both hands together, the space between them forming the rough shape of an oval, slightly pointed at each end.

'May the Sacred Eye watch over you,' he said solemnly.

Ildaron made the same sign.

'May its power protect you,' she murmured.

And taking Quen's hand, she led him away.

Quen had expected her to take one of the established paths. But instead, she went straight through the forest in a north-easterly direction. Surprisingly, he did not get scratched and torn as when he had followed the fox: it was as if she knew in advance where the forest was thinnest or where there were gaps between the tangle of bushes and trees. Time and again they would walk straight towards what looked like a solid barrier of thick undergrowth; but always at the last moment a narrow opening would appear, allowing them to pass through. Even after night had fallen this strange power didn't leave her. For some hours, Quen, holding tightly to the loose sleeve of her robe, stumbled blindly through the darkness – unable to see the sky, surrounded on all sides by the murmuring shadows of living vegetation.

Close to midnight, they emerged from the thick forest temporarily and stopped on a slight hillside which was covered with fragrant-smelling heather.

'We will rest here for a while,' Ildaron said softly.

Quen had felt oppressed by the constant overhang of foliage, and now, thankfully, he lay back on the heather and gazed up at the clear starry sky. Out of the corner of his eye, he saw the brief flash of a falling star and he recalled how Faya had said that that was always a good omen. Without quite knowing why, he reached down and touched the slight bulge in the hem of his tunic – the feel of the diamond, even through the layers of wool and cloth, was somehow warm and familiar and reassuring.

Before he could drift off into sleep, Ildaron gave him a handful of dried fruit and nuts to take the edge off his hunger. It was while he was eating these that he asked a question which had been on his mind for some time.

'I noticed,' he said, 'that Fraylon had no fear of the Mollag. Is it because they are powerless against you? Can they do you no harm?'

'We are not defenceless,' Ildaron replied. 'The power of the Eye is strong in us. But still it is true that the Mollag could harm us.'

'Then why do you not fear them?'

There was a brief silence during which an owl hooted mournfully.

'It is because we are the Pale Keepers – the Keepers of the Law. And the Law teaches us that in times of peril, when the sacred forest and its people are being threatened, One will come to save us from the danger.'

'Who is this One you speak of?' Quen asked.

'That we do not know. But we are taught he will be sent to us by the Wise Ones.'

Quen thought about this for a moment.

'You say that One will come to save us. But while you wait, look at what is happening: the Mollag have overrun the land. Can't you do something to help the people now?'

'We are doing what we have always done – we are upholding the Law. That is why you are here now: because you have broken that Law. We cannot control the Mollag, but we can and must govern the people placed in our care. Our duty is to rule over the people of the ten villages, to rule in the name of Thual, bringer of all.'

Quen hesitated before putting the next question: he knew that what he was about to say, under normal circumstances, would not be permitted.

'But is Thual really the greatest power in the land?' he asked uncertainly. 'Aren't the Wise Ones more important? You've said yourself that it is they who will send One to save Thual from the Mollag.'

Ildaron's voice, when she answered, was cold and disapproving.

'Nothing is greater than Thual, not even the Wise Ones.

Although they stand above us, they too are only servants of the forest. Thual is the bringer of fire and water, the preserver of earth and sky. Without it, there is nothing.'

Her closing words reminded Quen of his meeting with Nodak: the woodsman, too, had said very much the same. And now, apparently, he could look forward to One who would come to save them all. Who would that One be? And when would he arrive? As a promise, it worried Quen: it sounded too vague and uncertain, too much like a dream of the future – a mere bubble of hope compared with the visible and very real threat of the Mollag. Again Quen reached down and touched the hidden diamond for reassurance. And with the warm feel of it against his fingertips, he fell into a deep and restful sleep.

Ildaron woke him before dawn and again they hurried on. Although he had slept for only five hours, Quen found that he was fitter and stronger than he had been on the previous evening. The last traces of pain had disappeared and he had grown used to having one useless arm. Once again he felt balanced and relaxed, able to move freely and quickly through the forest.

With only short rest periods they continued their journey throughout the morning. At about midday they came to the edge of a shallow valley. Beyond the valley was a range of rocky hills which rose steeply up to jagged peaks. So steep were the upper slopes that they would probably have been impassable had there not been a narrow track cut out of the rock and winding up towards a natural pass between the lowest peaks. Quen could see the track quite clearly from where he lay hidden in the ferns at the forest's edge. Yet it was not that which attracted his attention. Immediately below him in the valley was a wooden tower built right beside the beginning of the track and guarded by two Mollag soldiers. It needed only a glance to tell him that nobody could possibly reach the track, least of all climb it, without being seen by the two guards. How then were he and Ildaron to continue?

He was puzzling over this problem when Ildaron touched him lightly on the shoulder. He turned and found himself staring into her wide open eyes. There was no time to back away or protest. Almost immediately he fell under her power: his own eyes became glazed and unseeing; his body was frozen into a fixed position. Yet although he looked exactly like a frozen statue and appeared to be completely under her control, still a small part of himself remained free and untouched – a tiny voice or self which crouched somewhere in the back of his mind, somehow hidden from the sight of Ildaron's probing eyes. That faint voice told him now to get up, to throw off Ildaron's power; but struggle as he might, he could not move nor break the spell. And from somewhere close by, so much more powerful than his own inner voice, almost drowning it out, he could hear Ildaron speaking to him.

'From this point onwards,' she was saying, 'you must continue on alone. I shall hold the guards long enough for you to pass by. Your task is to reach the entrance to the Caverns, which is beyond the seventh bend in the rocky track. Nothing must prevent your getting there, nothing. That is my command. Do you understand me?'

His body, rigid and stiff until then, relaxed slightly as he nodded his agreement – and then immediately froze once again.

'I shall now go down to the guards alone,' she went on, 'while you remain hidden. When I give the signal, you must run across to the track and up to the Caverns. I repeat: nothing must prevent you.'

The moment she stopped speaking, his own inner voice made itself heard again, telling him faintly not to obey. As though sensing that perhaps Quen was not completely in her power, Ildaron hesitated for a second or two.

'You have understood me?' she asked again, suspiciously.

He nodded, and without further delay she strode down the hillside to the tower. The guards saw her when she had covered less than half the distance. They slid down the centre pole of the tower and ran threateningly towards her, their eyes showing like black discs in their death-grey faces. But before they could reach her she fixed them with her stare and, like Quen, they were frozen in their tracks. Motioning with one hand, she called out:

'Now Quen, come. Hurry to the Caverns.'

Quen's still body leaped immediately into action. He jerked to his feet and ran stiffly down the slope. Without even glancing at the hated Mollag guards, he reached the lowest part of the track and began the steep winding climb. The small voice inside him told him to stop, to regain his freedom; but although it droned on and on, he could not prevent his legs moving, carrying him upwards.

He moved rapidly around the first of the seven bends, and then the second and the third. But as he approached the next long curve, he suddenly noticed a Mollag guard far up ahead and coming towards him. The Mollag must have seen him at the same time, because he gave a great roaring shout and came charging down the twisting track. In his fuddled state, Quen stood quite still for a moment, going neither forwards nor backwards. It seemed there was nowhere left for him to turn. As he hesitated, Ildaron's voice came crashing through the vacant spaces of his mind: 'Nothing must prevent your getting there, nothing. That is my command.' And without a flicker of fear, his eyes still glazed and unseeing, he turned towards the sheer rock hillside and, reaching for a handhold with his one good arm, slowly began to climb.

12 · The Caverns

FORTUNATELY for Quen, he retained very little memory of that long and hazardous climb. Under normal circumstances, he would have found it totally impossible to scale such a rock-face, especially with his left arm damaged. But in his strange trance-like condition he climbed almost like a robot, moving jerkily from one ledge to the next.

To begin with, the small voice inside him, faint but persistent, kept urging him to stop. But it seemed that nothing, not the danger nor the cries of protest, could reach whatever strange power it was that drove him. His body, blindly obedient to Ildaron's command, continued to struggle on; and soon, choked with terror and dismay, the inner voice grew silent.

After that he lost all sense of time and space. Like a fly on a vast grey-black surface, he worked his way slowly upwards until he was hundreds of feet above the track. At that height fierce winds buffeted him, wrenching at his hair and tunic, threatening to tear him from the hillside and send him spinning down to his death. Yet even this increased danger had no visible effect on him. In his mesmerized state, he saw the rock before him as the whole world. Nothing else penetrated his dazed consciousness; and it was as if he must go on climbing forever.

But there finally came a point when he stretched up, feeling for a handhold, and his groping fingers, instead of touching smooth rock, found a broad ledge. He had reached not the top of the towering hillside, but a narrow opening in the cliff. Ignoring a sudden gust of wind, he clambered onto this ledge and crawled through the narrow gap.

Right up until that moment he had continued to move mechanically. But now something bright and urgent, brighter even than the sun, flashed across his vision; and straight away the voice began once again to murmur within him, urging him to break free. There was a period of struggle, during which his face twitched uncontrollably. Then, slowly, as though guided by some unknown instinct, his hand groped down to where the diamond lay hidden in the hem of his tunic. Through the cloth he could feel the familiar rounded shape; and at its touch Ildaron's power fell away from him and he awoke.

He found himself in a wide chamber lit on four sides by thin slit openings which looked out over the surrounding forest. In the middle of this chamber was a huge oval table made of wood. It was no ordinary table: the whole of its large surface was pitted with shallow, dish-like hollows, each of them shaped approximately like an eye. There were hundreds of these eye-shaped hollows and in most of them there nestled a single brilliant diamond. The total effect was like looking at a cluster of eyes whose gleaming pupils caught the faint light from the slit windows and reflected it, dazzlingly, into the rest of the chamber. Clearly, this was what had helped to awaken him.

Quen crept forward to the edge of the table. The diamonds, like the eye-shaped hollows in which they rested, were of different sizes – some, tiny pin-pricks of light; others, fathomless pools of white and blue. Gazing into these larger stones made him feel as though he were sinking into deep sun-filled water. He tried to draw back, but it was too late. Already he was drifting down and down, with colour and shadow whirling around his head, enclosing him.

Yet this experience was nothing like the trance from which he had just emerged. Instead of deadening his consciousness, it seemed to heighten it. And for a few brief seconds he was transported beyond the present and into the future. In a series of fleeting visions, he caught glimpses of the journey which still lay before him: the autumn forest, sad with falling leaves; the forbidding craggy peaks of mountains higher than he would have thought possible; himself, grey-faced, cold and wretched, staggering blindly across a wintery snow-filled landscape; and finally his mother, Faya, pleading desperately with him not to betray his people. These visions alone might have terrified him, had it not been for what lay behind them. Always, hovering in the background, were the vague outlines of two mysterious faces. He could not see them clearly, yet somehow he knew they were smiling at him encouragingly, reassuring him, urging him on towards a goal which he could not quite grasp or understand.

Straining forward, Quen tried with all his might to bring these strange images into clearer focus; but almost as suddenly as they had appeared, so now they faded and vanished. And even as he shook his head in bewilderment, he found himself back in the hillside chamber, cut off from those friendly and encouraging presences which, just for a moment, had been so close to him. Never, it seemed, had he felt quite so alone. With a sigh, he turned away from the table, towards the single doorway in the far wall of the chamber – only to find himself confronted by a tall white-robed figure.

Quen did not even try to escape. The silent figure completely filled the narrow doorway. Moreover, Quen knew only too well the power of the Pale Keepers, and was not eager to test it unnecessarily. In silence, he allowed himself to be led from the chamber and along a dimly lit passage which had been carved through the rock. This passage wound steadily down, deep into the base of the hillside, ending at last in a spacious hall lit by flares.

A large number of the Pale Keepers was gathered there, as though waiting for him. All were dressed in the now familiar white robes and hat – all, that is, except for one old woman who sat on a raised platform at the end of the hall. She was bareheaded and dressed entirely in black, and her grey hair hung loose all around her thin wizened face. So thin and withered was her face, the skin wrinkled, the mouth sunken, that only her eyes still seemed alive. They were large and grey-blue, more like the eyes of a young woman, sharp and bright, fixed fiercely upon him from the moment he entered the hall.

As he paused just beyond the entrance, rapidly taking in this strange scene, she lifted one wasted hand and beckoned him forward. With lowered eyes he stepped up onto the platform and stood before her.

'You know why you are here?' she asked him, her surprisingly strong voice filling the hall.

He nodded, still without looking up.

'Very well,' she said. 'Then understand that it is I, Alron, oldest of the Pale Keepers, who will judge your unlawful behaviour. Have you anything to say on your own behalf?'

For the first time Quen looked up. He wanted to explain everything: the desperate state of things in the ten villages, the threat to his sister's life, what he hoped to achieve by his journey. But before he could begin he noticed an astonished expression on Alron's face; and as he opened his mouth to speak, she cut him short with a wave of her hand.

'Who is it who sent this boy to the Caverns?' she called out into the body of the hall.

Ildaron, unnoticed by Quen until that moment, stepped forward.

'It was I,' she said quietly.

'Was it not reported by you that this boy was under the spell of the Eye?'

'He was,' Ildaron asserted firmly.

'Yet now the spell is broken. See for yourself.'

The old withered hand reached out, grasped Quen roughly by the hair, and turned him to face the hall. There was a pause, followed by a murmur of surprise from the assembled Pale Keepers.

'How do you explain this?' she asked angrily.

'I do not understand it,' Ildaron said. 'When I placed the spell on him, I felt some resistance – but only a little. I am sure that the power was upon him.'

'Yet it is gone!' Alron exclaimed, her voice rising. 'Can the power simply disappear into the air? Is that what you are saying?'

Without waiting for a reply, she turned back to Quen.

'What can you tell us, boy?' she asked. 'What has happened to the spell Ildaron placed upon you? And give me no lies! I know that you are not one of the Chosen – you do not possess the secret of the Eye.'

Quen briefly considered telling her of the diamond he carried, of how the touch of it had awoken him. But he immediately dismissed the idea. Instead he answered:

'It is true that I am of the unchosen. But my presence here is not unlawful as you have said. I was sent into Thual by my mother, Faya, who has been taught your ways. She would not ask me to act against the spirit of the Law.'

'This is lies!' Alron burst out. 'I know Faya. It was I who taught her the ways of the Pale Keepers. She would not send you into the forest – not a boy who hunts, who tries to kill the beasts of Thual.'

'I admit that I have once hunted deer,' Quen said humbly. 'I still think of that time with shame. I now realize it was wrong. And yet . . .' he hesitated, '. . . and yet I don't understand this part of the Law. Why is it that man is punished for hunting within Thual, when creatures like the fox and hawk go free?'

The old woman shook her head impatiently.

'You are not here to question me,' she said. 'Your task is to obey. It is enough for you to know that man is forbidden to hunt in the forest. And you must now answer for your misdeed.'

'But I have already paid the penalty,' Quen protested, 'to Namu.'

'More lies . . .' Alron began, but before she could go on Ildaron again stepped forward.

'No, Alron,' she said. 'That is true. For I have seen with my own eyes how the boy travels with the fox.'

For the second time Alron showed surprise.

'With the fox?' she said, puzzled, her old forehead wrinkled and thoughtful. 'There are things here I do not understand. The time has come to sift the truth from any falsehood that may lie buried within it. Look at me, boy.'

So saying, she placed both bony hands on Quen's shoulders and gazed at him intently. Her eyes seemed to become larger and brighter. Somewhere in their depths Quen could see two minute points of light which grew steadily until he felt that he was looking at two shimmering diamonds floating in space. Slowly, these two shimmering surfaces moved together, and as they gradually merged into one, Quen began to lose all memory of who and where he was. Vaguely, he was aware that once that single shining gem had formed, blotting out all else, he, Quen, would cease to exist: he would be only a voice, able merely to chant out the events of some distant past. Furtively, with what little of his own will still remained, he felt along the hem of his tunic until his fingers encountered the hiding place of the diamond.

Once again it protected him. No sooner had he touched it than a warm centre, somewhere within himself, refused to submit. It, too, grew steadily, resisting the great shining gem which filled his vision. There was a short period, partly of confusion, partly of struggle, and suddenly the gem dissolved, shattering into a million fragments of fading light. As before Quen was standing in the flare-lit hall staring at the grey-blue eyes of Alron – though now the diamond beneath his fingers seemed to glow and throb, to send currents of warmth and strength through his hand and arm and into the rest of his body.

There was again a murmur of amazement throughout the hall. Alron continued to watch him intently. Without taking her eyes from his face, she called out:

'Where was this boy found?'

A voice from amongst the Pale Keepers answered:

'He was found hiding within the Chamber of the Eye.'

'Then you have added to your crimes,' Alron said menacingly. 'For you have stolen one of the sacred stones. There is no other way that you could have resisted my power. Give it to me, boy' – and she held one hand out towards him.

Before he could stop himself, Quen blurted out:

'No! I have stolen nothing! The stone is mine, my own sign, given to me by my mother.'

'There is one way of testing the truth of your words,' Alron said softly, 'and that is for you to show us the stone. The stone itself will not lie.'

Dumbly, Quen tore open part of the hem of his tunic, took out the small bag, and slipped the diamond into the palm of his hand, allowing it to sparkle and shine within full view. This time there was a gasp of sheer astonishment from all the watchers in the hall and a voice called out: 'It has not dulled! See! It has not dulled!'

Alron, also, was taken aback, but she still regarded him suspiciously.

'Do you dare actually to hold the stone in your hand,' she asked slowly, 'and to say again that it is yours?'

'I have not stolen it,' Quen stated firmly. 'It belonged to my mother, but she gave it to me freely, and now it is mine.'

Alron watched the diamond intently as he spoke, as though she expected it to change in some way; but it continued to shine as brightly as ever. With a baffled sigh, she leaned back.

'It has not dulled,' she said to the expectant audience. 'The stone bears out the truth of his words.'

Now there was no sound from the Pale Keepers: all were waiting to see what Alron would decide. The old woman carefully rearranged her black robes, pondering silently before she spoke.

'We are ready to hear your story,' she said at last. 'Tell us what has brought you into Thual.'

Quen took a deep breath.

'The people of the ten villages have been enslaved by the Mollag,' he began. 'They need help to drive . . ..'

But Alron cut in on him sharply.

'All this we know. We are not sitting here helplessly: we are waiting for the One who will rid the forest of the Mollag.'

'The people have grown tired of waiting,' Quen said quickly. 'That is why I am here: I have been sent to find the Wise Ones, Keepers of the Sacred Eye.'

'And what do you propose to do when you have found them?' Alron asked him almost slyly.

'My mother has said that the Eye alone can consume the Mollag. That is our hope. With it, I could return to the coast and confront Ungeth, the Mollag leader.'

An expression very close to amusement passed across the old woman's face.

'Then I must tell you,' she said deliberately, 'that your journey is as foolish as it is brave.'

'Why do you call it foolish?' Quen asked.

'Because what you seek is already in your hand. That diamond which you claim is yours is part of the Sacred Eye.'

Quen opened his hand and looked anew at the glowing gem.

'This?' he said, unbelieving.

Alron nodded.

'Long ago,' she explained, 'the Sacred Eye existed here, within the Caverns. How it came to be shattered only the Wise Ones know. But what you now possess is part of that huge stone.'

Dumbfounded, Quen said nothing.

'Have you lost your tongue then?' Alron asked. 'Come, boy, you have been talkative enough so far. Tell us, what do you propose to do now?'

Quen shuffled his feet uncomfortably.

'I don't know,' he admitted. 'I need time to think about what you have said.'

'The boy speaks wisely,' Alron said, addressing the Pale Keepers once again. 'We, too, would do well to think about what has happened. Clearly, this child is not simply an intruder into Thual. His rightful possession of the stone, even though he is not one of the Chosen, and the fact that he was accompanied by the fox – these are things which should make us pause. We will meet here again tomorrow. In the meantime we will consider our decision.'

The Pale Keepers immediately began to disperse and Quen was taken to a tiny cell high in the hillside. There was a narrow window in the room, but it was too far above his head for him to see out, and left to himself he lay down on the bed and tried to make sense of what had happened. His mother had told him that the Sacred Eye would consume their enemies; and yet Alron claimed that the Eye had been broken into small fragments like the one he carried. Was that perhaps a clue to the old saying which Faya and Nodak had told him: that the Eye could be grasped but never possessed? Perhaps. But then, if the Eye was shattered and could not be taken back to the ten villages, how could it possibly destroy the power of Ungeth? Were all his efforts so far simply a wild-goose chase? And if that were so, why had he experienced a vision of the future up there in the Chamber of the Eye? A future, what is more, in which he continued with his journey?

By nightfall, exhausted by such questions, Quen thankfully gave himself up to sleep. He told himself that the next day, when he was rested, would be the time for decisions. But throughout the following morning he continued to feel baffled, and when he was again taken down to face Alron he had still not made up his mind.

The old woman, however, was far more decisive.

'We have thought long and hard about your presence in Thual,' she said, 'and we have decided that it is lawful for you to be here – for two reasons: because of your ownership of the sacred stone; and because we now see that you were misled. Both you and Faya mistakenly believed in what no longer exists, and for that you may be forgiven.'

Her judgment seemed straightforward enough and should have come as a relief, yet strangely it troubled Quen. He sensed that what worried him most were her closing words, the part about Faya being mistaken when in fact she had appeared so certain.

'You say the Sacred Eye no longer exists,' he said.

Alron nodded.

'And the Wise Ones? Are we also mistaken in believing in them?'

'No,' Alron said severely. 'They are the Great Keepers. Somewhere within Thual they lie hidden; they will reveal themselves when the time is ripe. It is they who will send the One to save us.'

Here, at last, was something sure upon which Quen could act. For suddenly he remembered his vision in the Chamber of the Eye – how the two kindly faces had appeared dimly before him, watching over him as he journeyed onward.

'Then I must go on,' he said confidently. 'There can be no further talk of mistakes or of turning back, for my journey is to the Wise Ones.'

'But I have told you,' Alron argued, 'the Sacred Eye no longer exists, not as a single stone. And you, a mere boy, cannot hope to find the Wise Ones.'

'Perhaps,' he said, 'but I must try just the same.'

Alron shook her finger at him warningly.

'Listen to an old woman,' she began, 'be advised and remain here in safety . . ..' She stopped, seeing from the set of his face that his mind was made up. 'Very well,' she added, 'we will not prevent your journey.'

'I ask more than permission to continue,' Quen said. 'I need your help. The track outside is heavily guarded by Mollag soldiers. Is there another way across the hills?'

'There is only one other way,' she said, 'and that is through the tunnel of black water. But it would be especially hazardous now.'

'I have no choice,' Quen replied. 'Hazardous or not, I must take it.'

13 · Dark Passage

THE TUNNEL of black water, Quen learned, lay further up the track. At the ninth bend a steep and narrow stairway, carved in the rock, led down into the valley. Just above the valley floor a stream flowed straight out of the hillside; and it was the tunnel in the rock made by this stream which Quen had to reach.

His main problem was how to get to the head of the stairway without being seen, and his first idea was to leave at night. But the Mollag knew he was sheltering with the Pale Keepers, and each evening, soon after sunset, soldiers were sent to guard the entrance to the Caverns. This meant that he had to leave by day, and he chose as the best possible time the short period immediately before sunrise, when the light was still uncertain and tinged with grey.

The following morning, as soon as the Mollag guards had marched back down the track, the heavy Cavern door was opened just wide enough for him to slip outside. All around him the dawn atmosphere was cool and still. Keeping close to the inner wall of the track, Quen crept cautiously uphill. He knew he had the advantage of the Mollag guarding the upper pass: for whereas he could see them clearly outlined against the brightening sky, they were looking down into the shadowy valley.

With this in mind, he worked his way quickly around the first of the two bends. It was still several minutes before sunrise and the morning remained calm and still. Ahead of him the track bent inwards, winding further into the hillside. Once in that deeper shade, he would for a time be invisible from above. But just as he was about to enter this shaded area, something suddenly leaped up before him. He had a startled impression of long spidery arms and legs, of a thin probing nose and grey silvery discs of eyes – and then the silence of the early morning was shattered by shrill mournful cries. He had no opportunity to look more carefully at the creature that had surprised him. The Mollag guards were already on the alert in the pass above and he had no time to waste.

Following the thin shadowy form that loped on ahead, he sped up the track as fast as he could. But now two guards were lumbering down towards him. Gasping for breath, he reached the head of the narrow staircase and leaped down it, almost falling in his haste. To his left, he could see the tunnel opening, where the stream bubbled from the hillside. Keeping within the partial shelter of a few straggly bushes, he sprinted for this opening. By then the guards, shouting with cruel excitement, had started to descend the staircase. Too late, they realized what he was doing and they flung their spears in a last desperate attempt to stop him. But before the heavy metal heads clattered against the rocky slope, he had disappeared into the worn tunnel of the stream.

Within a few yards the tunnel narrowed to such an extent that, as he squirmed between the smooth rocks, he knew the thick-set guards could not possibly follow him. Just the same, he pressed on to a point where the tunnel was large enough for him to stand up. By then he was in total darkness and had to feel his way along with one hand on the rock beside him.

It was an eerie and frightening sensation, walking through complete blackness with no sense of direction, the cool water washing against his feet. Yet even that sensation was preferable to what followed. He had been groping forward for some time when unexpectedly the rock disappeared beneath him and he stepped into deep cold water which seemed to clasp at his body, swiftly drawing him down and closing over his head.

Struggling with his one free arm, he fought his way back to the surface and clutched at the rocky ledge he had just left. It would have been easy enough for him to pull himself out. But what was the use? To go back meant capture. He had to follow the tunnel at all costs.

After a short rest he explored the pool into which he had fallen. In the thick darkness, he had imagined it as huge, almost limitless, and was surprised to find that it was only a few yards across. On the far side there was no tunnel, only a sheer smooth face of rock. Rightly, though not without a shuddering sense of dread, Quen guessed that the pool continued under the rock and that to go forward he would have to dive deep into the inky water. But how deep? And how far would he have to swim before he again reached the air-filled tunnel?

There was only one way to answer such questions, and mustering his failing courage he sank beneath the surface and kicked himself free of the rock.

How far he swam, he never knew. He remembered reaching a certain point where he almost gave up – that point beyond which there was no hope of turning back. But after only a fraction of hesitation, he continued forwards. For a space of unmeasurable time cold water slid past his face, and whenever he reached up his hand encountered solid rock. He felt his lungs bursting and the air he could no longer hold in trailing across his cheeks in a stream of bubbles. And then, before he could drag water into his lungs, the rock disappeared, he thrust himself upwards, his head breaking the surface, and he was again drawing in deep breaths.

He found himself in another small pool. It looked much the same size as the one he had just left, and yet at the same time there was something peculiarly different about it. In his dizzy, breathless state he could not quite place this difference; and he was still struggling dimly to understand it when strong hands grasped him by the shoulders, pulled him clear of the water, and set him down on a dry shelf of rock.

He understood then why everything appeared so oddly changed: he was no longer in total darkness. In a corner of the long tunnel-like cave a lamp was burning, casting its yellow light over the smooth water-worn walls of rock. With a feeling of relief, Quen saw the small prick-eared head of the fox watching him, and he turned, expecting to find Namu. But instead, he found himself looking at Nodak.

'What are you doing here?' Quen gasped out, astonished at finding the woodsman in such a place, deep beneath the ground.

'This is the only unguarded passage through the hills,' Nodak said. 'I knew that if the Pale Keepers released you, you would have to take it. And so I came here and waited.'

'But why did you wish to see me at all?' Quen asked.

'I come from Namu, who again sends you the fox to guide you safely through the forest.' He indicated the small creature crouching patiently nearby. 'But also I come to learn the fate of your precious stone. Have the Pale Keepers taken it from you?'

'No, I have it still' – and Quen held up the cloth bag which now hung from a cord at his neck. 'The Pale Keepers accepted that it was mine.'

'Did they tell you what it means? Where it came from?'

Quen nodded.

'Alron explained that it was part of the Sacred Eye which was shattered long ago.'

Nodak looked at him with a puzzled frown on his aging face.

'You know all this,' he said, 'and yet still you go on. I don't understand. What is there to search for?'

'There are still the Wise Ones,' Quen answered.

Nodak sighed and sat down on the rock beside him.

'Listen to me, Quen,' he said quietly. 'Alron has told you truly that the Sacred Eye is broken. Now I tell you that the Wise Ones do not exist. Not any longer. You are wasting your time; you are risking your life hunting for people who live on only in the old stories. Give up your search. Return to the villages where you might yet be safe. That is why the fox is here now, to guide you back.'

At Nodak's words, Quen felt a chill pang of disappointment.

'But how do you know the Wise Ones no longer dwell somewhere in Thual?' he broke out.

'Think, Quen,' Nodak insisted, 'remember the old sayings which your mother and I repeated to you – how the Wise Ones are hidden in the Eye. They are not people: they were the power that dwelt within the Eye itself; and now that the sacred stone is broken, its great power is lost. That is why we are told that the Eye can be grasped but never possessed. Like the Wise Ones, the power of the sacred stone is gone forever.'

'But these are only words and arguments,' Quen cried desperately. 'How can you be sure that the Wise Ones are not alive somewhere, in spite of everything you say?'

Nodak put his hand sadly on the boy's shoulder.

'Because I have looked for them myself,' he said. 'Nobody knows the forest better than I. Many years ago I crossed the hills and explored as far as the desert mountains, where nothing lives. There were no Wise Ones, Quen: only a few old charcoal burners and farmers who lived at the forest's edge, close to the desert. And they, for all I know, may be dead and gone by now.'

'Then there is no help for the villages?' Quen asked miserably. 'Nothing to save my sister Arla from the Mollag?'

'There is only the help we can give,' Nodak said. 'That is why we must go back.'

Quen sat quietly for some time, staring thoughtfully at the ground. It was possible that what Nodak said was true. And yet in spite of all his fears, he could not bring himself to believe the woodsman. Hadn't he, Quen, looked briefly into the future and seen the dim outline of those two kindly faces watching over him? How then could Nodak be right? Were those faces merely a part of his imagination? Or did they really exist? Were they waiting for him somewhere in the outermost parts of Thual?

With sudden decision, Quen stood up and faced the woodsman.

'No,' he said, 'you must go back alone. I am a boy; I lack the strength of a man; and I know from experience that I can do nothing in the villages. The only possible help I can give the villages is here in Thual. While there is even the faintest hope of finding the Wise Ones I must go on.'

'If that is your decision,' Nodak murmured, 'then I shall say nothing more.' And he picked up the lamp and led the way along the winding tunnel of the stream.

With the lamp to guide them, they completed the journey

quickly and safely and soon emerged on the far side of the hills. Nodak led him back up the hillside until they could look out right over Thual. In the distance the mountains glinted white and mauve in the sunlight.

'The desert begins in the foothills of the mountains,' Nodak explained. 'But I advise you now, there is very little chance of your ever getting that far, because the Mollag have brought the Chasers to hunt you down.'

'The Chasers?' Quen asked.

'They are long thin creatures which they use for tracking.'

Quen remembered the spidery figure leaping out on him in the early morning.

'Yes,' he said, 'I have seen them already.'

'Even the fox cannot protect you from them for long,' Nodak warned. 'They follow any trail.'

Quen shrugged.

'It makes no difference,' he said.

And after a brief farewell, he and the fox threaded their way down the hillside towards the waiting forest.

14 · Destruction

FOR three days there were no signs of pursuit and Quen travelled in peace. But the summer was almost ended: the leaves were changing colour and falling; a thin cold wind had begun blowing through the forest. And on the fourth day he stopped long enough to cut dry bark from a tree and to tie it around his body as protection from the wind. That, it seems, was his first error. The marked tree must have been too clear a sign, because from then on the Mollag were on his trail.

Throughout the daylight hours, and even at night, when he lay curled up, cold and tired, within a bank of fallen leaves, he would hear the Chasers calling shrilly somewhere in the forest. And no matter how the fox backtracked and followed the stony beds of streams, always those cries grew steadily closer.

One Chaser in particular was never far behind him. He learned to recognize its distinctive cry – a high-pitched piercing call almost like a scream. Its familiar sound would shatter the silence of the forest at any time of day or night. Quen might be foraging for food or lying asleep, and immediately he would start to his feet and run off.

One day he even saw the creature. The fox had backtracked and stopped in a thick clump of bushes. Through the yellowing leaves Quen spied the Chaser go padding by – a tall angular figure, deathly pale, with arms and legs like twigs, its dull silver eyes and long pointed nose close to the ground. Not far behind came the Mollag soldier, following the Chaser as a man might follow a dog.

Quen realized then that he could not hold out much longer. Even the fox's cleverest manoeuvres barely kept the enemy at bay long enough for him to sleep. And as for food, he had to be content with the withered berries and nuts which he could snatch from the bushes as he ran past. Soon he was groggy and tired, able to keep going only through an act of will; and he would almost certainly have given himself up if it had not been for something which happened late one afternoon.

Throughout that day they had only just managed to stay ahead of their pursuers. Time and again the piercing cry had sounded right behind them, and always the fox had contrived somehow to rescue them from capture at the last moment. In the fading evening light it had succeeded yet again, and for the second time Quen hid in a clump of bushes as the Chaser and, soon afterwards, the Mollag ran past. On this occasion the soldier was not merely following: his mouth was stretched wide and he was letting out hoarse cries of rage.

That put new heart in Quen – the realization that he was angering the soldier by constantly keeping one step ahead – and he determined to keep going until he dropped. But the Mollag's anger also gave him something more than determination: it formed the basis of a plan which offered him his first real hope of escape.

The plan occurred to him later that same night. Quen was following the bobbing brush along the moonlit paths when suddenly the fox stopped and sniffed the ground. It was similar to what had happened once before, and this time Quen did not act rashly. Picking up a small stick, he carefully pushed aside the fallen leaves on the path, expecting to uncover a net. But instead, he discovered a metal trap; and a few yards further on, another. Behind him, Quen could hear the Chaser calling and see a glimmer of light made by the burning torch which the Mollag carried. His immediate impulse was to spring the traps and hurry on. But then he remembered the Mollag's anger and his earlier realization that cunning alone could save him. Here, perhaps, was the time to use that cunning, when the Mollag was no longer thinking clearly, his mind blinded by anger and frustration.

Taking care not to set off the traps, Quen covered them again with fallen leaves. The fox, meanwhile, aware of the danger behind, was impatient to be off. But before the small creature could dart away down the path, Quen grasped it by its soft fur and picked it up, cradling it with his right arm. By then the Chaser and the guard, running almost together, were very nearly upon them. Yet still Quen didn't move: he waited until he had actually been seen before leaping off into the dark.

Now the cries behind him were louder than ever. Nor did he even try to outdistance the Mollag. Keeping to the heavy undergrowth so as to confuse his pursuers' sense of direction, he worked his way round in a complete circle. Those last few yards were critical – he could not allow the Mollag any opportunity to think or to assess the situation – and when he finally rejoined the track both Chaser and Mollag were only yards behind. Immediately ahead of him lay the area of path which the fox had sniffed at so suspiciously, and with two bounds Quen was across it safely. But not so the figures behind him. There were two vicious snaps, one after the other, and his hunters were firmly caught in their own traps.

It was at that moment, when he was flushed with success, that Quen made his biggest mistake. Instead of using the opportunity to escape, he stopped and laughed aloud with triumph. And the Mollag, unable to move, his right leg crushed and held by the vice-like jaws, roared out in rage and pain and hurled the burning torch at Quen's head. He easily managed to dodge out of the way, and the torch (as he thought) spun harmlessly away into the bushes.

But after the long dry summer, there was nothing harmless about a burning brand. The autumn leaves were as dry as tinder and within seconds long tongues of flame were licking up through the undergrowth. Quen tried to stamp them out, but he was too late, and in an astonishingly short time he was driven back by the heat from a growing wall of flame.

Within minutes it was as if the whole forest were alight. The fox, whimpering with fear, began squirming against him, and Quen put the animal down and followed it into the night. Behind them, the flames rose higher and higher, a straight line of flickering destruction marching through the forest at incredible speed. Both boy and fox ran as they had never run before, while all around them squirrels and small creatures fled before the advancing flames.

Soon it was as if the night had gone. The fire filled the air with a bright orange light in which great black clouds of smoke billowed upwards and large smuts of burning foliage floated and danced. Quen, his face smeared with ash and soot, his back hot from the fierce blaze, fled for his life. Yet despite his fear and the growing heat, he did not run blindly. He knew that his only real hope of survival lay with the fox and always he kept that small sinewy body in view.

Twice during that long fearful race, the fox led him down to shallow streams. Against smaller fires, they might have offered some protection, but against this giant of heat and smoke they were useless. What Quen needed was deep water, and it was clear from the way the fox followed every downward slope that this was what its clever little mind was seeking.

Glancing backwards, Quen could see that they didn't have much longer in which to search. The fire, which had been a straight wall of flame, had now formed into a great curve; it was like the broken hoop of a circle which was gradually closing in on them. Breathless and hot, Quen paused at the top of a rise. All around him the fire raged, leaving only the downward slope before him free of flame. The fox, after a brief turn of the head, bounded down through the tinder dry ferns. Already, burning fragments of leaf and twig were falling into the ferns, creating jets of flickering flame, and Quen, conscious that this was their last chance before the circle of fire totally enclosed them, leaped after the tiny animal.

But he need not have been afraid. The fox had never failed him in the past – nor did it now. For at the bottom of the slope, in the lowest part of the valley, was the remains of a lake. After the summer drought, it was no longer wide or deep; but still it was sufficient to protect them, and both Quen and the fox ran splashing through the shallows, swimming out into the centre where they both clung to a floating log.

There were many other creatures with them in the lake – deer, snakes, and a host of small mammals – and together they watched as the fire raged around the shore and rapidly moved away towards the east.

Nothing moved for a long time after that; and when the day eventually dawned it lit a dismal scene: the forest reduced to a grey smouldering ruin; wisps of smoke curling up from the charred remains of trees, and the ground thick with ash. Except for the cold and frightened faces which showed above the surface of the lake, no living thing was visible for miles around.

Looking at this scene of terrible destruction, Quen, for the second time during his journey, felt overcome by guilt and shame. He couldn't escape the conviction that this was partly his doing. If he had only listened to Nodak and turned back. If he had not been so vain and foolish as to stand laughing at the Mollag soldier everything might have been different. Whereas now, the forest which had sheltered and protected him so faithfully was reduced to this.

None of the animals had made any attempt to leave the lake – the floor of the forest was far too hot to walk on. But Quen was so filled with regret that he could not remain still. As on a previous occasion, he felt that this needless destruction had somehow to be paid for, and with the fox paddling after him, he swam to the lake's edge. There he pulled away the strips of bark which protected him from the cold and wound them round and round his feet. Then, with only this slight protection from the still smouldering ash, he stepped up onto the shore.

The fox, fearing to be left behind, gave its short nervous bark, but Quen paid it no attention. He felt that he was no longer worthy of such a companion – and in any case, until the earth cooled, the fox, like all the other animals, would be safer in the water. He alone had given up his right to any such refuge. And with this conviction, tired as he was, he turned once more to the east and began running through the desolate remains of the forest.

94

Even before he had covered the first mile the heat from the ash had penetrated the wet bark and begun burning and blistering his feet. But he refused to stop, running doggedly on towards the mountains as though he were trying to escape from himself, the person he felt so ashamed of. While behind him the morning breeze, playing over the burned floor of the forest, stirred the light ash and wiped out his faint footprints.

By late in the morning he had passed through the burned portion of the forest and reached the foothills of the mountains which rose, dry and forbidding, high above him. He was tired and hungry, his feet burned and sore, his face and hair blackened and singed by the fire on the previous night. The surrounding forest had become visibly thinner, with only the occasional tall tree, and this told him plainly that he was nearing the beginnings of the desert.

Just the thought of the desert reminded him of Nodak's words – how there used to be farmers working the land on the very fringes of the forest. He pictured to himself a small farm nestling in a valley. Since his recent failure, he had given up all his great hopes of finding sacred stones and wise people. Now, all he longed for was a humble place of refuge, a quiet farm of the sort Nodak had referred to. And no sooner had he voiced to himself this simple longing than he topped a shallow rise and found, directly below him in a peaceful green valley, exactly the kind of small farm which he had imagined.

An old man and woman were working in the garden beside a rambling overgrown hut and they looked up as he came stumbling down the green meadow. After the horrors of the past week, Quen felt that he had never seen such kindly, smiling faces. To his tired eyes they were like something from a dream, like some happy episode from a past he had never actually experienced, and with a sigh he stopped beside the hut door and waited as they came walking slowly towards him.

15 · Refuge

THE OLD man and his wife were poor people who lived only on what they could grow in the small clearing in the valley. From the outset, Quen warned them of the danger they would be in if they harboured him, of how the Mollag might harm them also; but they appeared completely untroubled by all his talk of violence and invasion.

'This is all we have,' the old woman said humbly, indicating the tiny farmlet. 'What do we have to fear from thieves and invaders? In any case,' she added, 'the forest will protect us as it always has done.'

And strangely, Quen came to accept her sense of peace and calm. At the back of his mind he still knew that the Mollag might arrive any day; and yet, disappointed and weary as he was, he found it impossible to resist the placid, peaceful atmosphere of the farm. So that despite his fears, he began to feel secure and safe there.

The old couple would not hear of his helping them.

'You need rest after your long journey,' the woman said kindly.

And each morning she put soothing ointments on his blistered feet and broken arm, while the man made a couch of soft heather for him. By then it was full autumn, with the trees changing colour, the leaves drifting down in the cool breeze which blew from the north; and Quen would lie outside the hut in the pale sunlight and watch the old people as they tended the land.

It was on just such a morning that he saw the fox once more. There was a slight movement at the edge of the forest and its sharp pointed face came thrusting through the foliage. From then on it appeared every day, but never once did it venture into the clearing or show signs of recognizing Quen who called to it from below. Puzzled, Quen finally mentioned its appearance to the old couple.

'What business would it have here?' the man said. 'Its place is in the forest. It is part of the vast cycle of life which protects us from the desert.'

Although he was not wholly satisfied with the answer, Quen said nothing more for a time, content to watch and wait.

His patience was rewarded soon afterwards. One afternoon the fox, which lay crouched in the long grass at the top of the meadow, gave its familiar nervous bark and disappeared. Minutes later, the long silvery-eyed face of a Chaser peered between the faded autumn leaves, apparently searching the valley. Quen, who had been about to get up and re-enter the hut, froze into fearful stillness as the cold eyes swept slowly over the peaceful scene. With every passing second he expected to hear the shrill cry which would alert the Mollag who followed. But like the fox, this creature also seemed blind to what lay in the valley, and as silently as it had appeared, the thin grey face withdrew.

Nonetheless, Quen suddenly felt spurred into action. He saw clearly that by remaining where he was, he could only bring death or capture onto these old people who had treated him so gently and well. Rising quickly from the heather couch, he stole quietly around the hut with the intention of creeping away. But before he was even half-way up the slope, the woman called out and came over to him, her old eyes twinkling happily.

'We also have seen the creature,' she said, 'but I have told you, no harm will come to you here. We are too old and poor in this valley to be noticed.'

And taking Quen gently by the arm she led him back to the hut

– where, as she had said, he did feel safe from harm, in spite of all that he knew of the cruelty of the Mollag.

After that the Chaser, like the fox, appeared each day, its dull silvery eyes blindly scanning the clearing. Although Quen no longer feared it, its presence troubled him; and on the fourth day, after the evening meal, when he and the old people were sitting around the warm fire, he asked them why it was that the valley protected them.

Instead of answering directly, the old man smiled quietly to himself.

'The protection does not come from this valley,' he said. 'There is nothing magical here.'

'Then why is it that we are not attacked?' Quen asked.

'Think,' the old man said. 'Put yourself in the place of the Chaser. What is it that he is searching for?'

Quen pondered the question for a moment.

'He is searching for someone who is frightened and weary,' he said hesitantly, 'for a boy who is constantly running and hiding.'

'And the fox?' the old man asked. 'What does he look for each day?'

'He is looking for the same person,' Quen answered.

'And now ask yourself whether such a person exists here,' the old man said, laughing again. 'Are you frightened and weary? Do you run and hide all the time? When the Chaser appears, do you tremble and try to escape?'

'No, I feel safe here, with you.'

'Then that is why they fail to see you,' the old man explained. 'Each day they feel drawn to this place because they sense you are near. But their minds are filled with an image of a frightened, tired boy who runs and tries to escape. They can think of nothing else. And because they cannot find such a person in this peaceful valley, they see nothing.'

'I'm not sure if I understand you,' Quen said, bewildered.

'What is there to understand? All I'm saying is that people can only see what already exists in their own minds. In the cruel and greedy minds of the Mollag there is no place for peace, contentment, and the absence of fear – which is why this valley puzzles and blinds them.'

'But I saw the valley,' Quen objected. 'I was not blinded or puzzled by it.'

'Ah yes,' the old woman broke in, smiling at him in the dim firelight, 'but what was in your mind as you came hurrying through the forest?'

Quen still had a vivid recollection of that morning. He clearly remembered how he had given up all hope of completing his journey, how he had imagined to himself a peaceful farm in which to take refuge – and how it was only then that the valley with its peaceful meadows had appeared before him.

'Now do you understand?' the old woman said quietly, as though reading what was in his mind. 'This place is what you were seeking, and so your eyes were opened.'

Quen asked no more questions that night, but throughout the next day he puzzled over all that had been spoken. When they were again seated around the fire in the fading evening light, he said:

'As you know, I have crossed the forest and come here, to the very edge of the desert, looking for the Wise Ones. You are older than I and understand many things. Can you, then, tell me this? Have I failed in my journey because the Wise Ones do not exist? This is what Nodak the woodsman has said. Or have I failed because I have not known where and how to look? Are my eyes, like those of the Mollag, blind?'

The old people said nothing for some time, while all around them, on the mud walls of the hut, the orange glow of the firelight flickered restlessly. Finally, the old man said quietly:

'That is a question which nobody may answer but yourself. All I can tell you is that you are not the first person to make such a journey. Nor, probably, will you be the last. The old stories speak of another who made just such a journey long ago.'

'And did he succeed?' Quen asked.

'Yes, he succeeded.'

'I should like to hear of that journey,' Quen said.

The old man glanced inquiringly across at the woman. She smiled and nodded and, settling herself comfortably on the wooden bench, began the story:

'Long ago,' she said, her voice soft and controlled, 'the forest of Thual covered the whole land. In those days the ten villages did not exist, nor the desert, nor the Pale Keepers. The forest was the home of every living creature and men shared it with the rest of the animals. The people were hunters then, as free to kill for food as the fox and the hawk, and there was plenty for everyone.

'But gradually some of the people became dissatisfied. They were not content with the simple lives they led; they wanted more. The same cruelty and greed which you have witnessed in the Mollag began to show itself in the lives of the ordinary people. Instead of merely hunting for food, they killed for the sake of killing. And soon they were not only hunting animals, but each other, and war raged across Thual. Beasts and men were slaughtered, the trees were burned and chopped down to build fortresses, whole regions were destroyed. It was then that the great desert began.

'In the midst of all this war and destruction, a young man set out on a journey. Like you, he had heard of the Wise Ones and of a sacred stone so powerful that it could bring peace to the forest once again. His adventures and the dangers he faced and overcame are too numerous to tell here; it is enough to say that at last he succeeded in finding the Wise Ones who directed him to a cave in the mountains. In that cave were many large magical stones, each of which possessed some special power. There was the stone of desire, the stone of peace, the stone of fear, and many more. But the young man was blind to all but one of them. In his mind he carried a single idea: he dreamed of a knowledge so complete and powerful that with it he could control every creature of the forest – do away with war and bring sanity back into Thual once again. And so, when he entered the mountain cave, he perceived only what became known as the Sacred Eye, the stone of seeing.

'This stone he took back with him to the forest. Nobody now could stand against him. With the Eye to help him, he could see everything that was going to happen. So powerful was he that with a single glance or a few words he could control a whole army. And soon he had persuaded the people to go back to their peaceable ways.

'But the Sacred Eye, which gave peace to everyone else, brought him only misery. For with it he could see everything; not only the good things, but all the grief and cruelty which existed in the world. It plagued him with visions of the past and future, and robbed him of sleep and rest. Sometimes he even caught glimpses of his own eventual death. But what concerned him most of all was the worry of what might happen when the stone passed into other hands. He understood clearly that it could be used not only to bring about good, but also evil. With the stone to help him, a person could plunge Thual into the bloodiest war of all.

'This fear possessed him so strongly that one day he climbed a steep hillside and threw the Sacred Eye down onto the rocks below – where it shattered into a thousand pieces.

'The great seeing power of the Eye was lost – though a small portion of its strength remained locked in each of the tiny fragments. It is those fragments which are now kept safely by the Pale Keepers. With the stones to help them, they made the people leave the forest, where their old hunting ways might again lead to war, and persuaded them to live peaceably on the narrow coastal plain.'

The old woman finished her story and looked at Quen who was fingering the stone in its cloth bag. It seemed to glow between his fingertips as if in response to some secret presence hidden somewhere in the lowly hut. Meanwhile a hundred questions came swarming into Quen's mind.

'Most of this I understand,' he said. 'But one thing more than any other remains unexplained. How did the young man find the Wise Ones?'

Now it was the old man who replied:

'The ancient stories tell us that throughout most of his wanderings he looked in the wrong way, he expected the wrong things. Only when he allowed the Wise Ones to present themselves in their own way, when he expected nothing, did he discover them.'

There was a pause, and then the old man added:

'What did you expect, Quen? What was it that you thought to find?'

Quen didn't answer immediately. He recalled how, in the back of his mind, he had imagined the Wise Ones inhabiting great mansions or palaces – even magical castles. But not this.

'Why here?' he broke out, amazed and fearful. 'Why only a simple hut and a farm?'

'Is there anything else?' the old man replied. 'What is wisdom if it is not the ability to live and work in peace and contentment?'

'Ah, now I understand!' Quen cried.

'Tell us what it is you understand,' the old man said quietly – but suddenly he and the woman were neither old nor young: they sat before him, ageless.

'I understand that I have found the Wise Ones,' Quen answered, and he fell forward, touching his forehead on the earth floor at their feet.

Immediately, a hand touched him gently on the shoulder, and he heard a voice whisper:

'Welcome, Quen, welcome.'

16 · The Eye of Desire

THAT night Quen lay on his bed thinking of all that had happened to him. In spite of the danger and the doubt and hardship, he had found the Wise Ones and he understood at last the meaning of the strange prophecy – how the Wise Ones were hidden in the Eye. He had imagined that they somehow dwelt within the Sacred Eye itself, whereas the truth was far simpler. It was not the precious stone which protected them, but the blindness of those who came to search. The valley and the old couple were here for anyone to see, yet people passed by because, like himself, they came looking for something else, something far grander and more magnificent. They could not appreciate what lay before their eyes, and it was this blindness which hid the Wise Ones and made of them such a mystery.

With these thoughts, Quen fell into a deep sleep. When he awoke, it was broad daylight and to his amazement his arm was completely healed. As he sat up, feeling fresh and strong once again, he saw the Wise Ones standing patiently at his bedside.

'The time has come to complete your journey,' the old man said, smiling at him kindly.

Quen would have liked to stay longer in the valley, but he rose without argument and made ready to leave. On the wooden bench were a thick wool-lined jacket and gloves, and a haversack filled with dried food and a flint and steel for making fire.

'Those are to help you on your way,' the woman said.

Quen thanked her and went outside with the old couple. The air was fresh and still and filled with the smells of late autumn. Above them, to the east, towered the great peaks of the mountains – to Quen they had never looked so large.

'At the far end of the meadow,' the man said, 'you will find a path. Follow it high into the mountains and on the fourth day you will come to a cave which contains the thing you are seeking. There is no great danger on this journey, but you must hurry because winter is close and soon there will be snow.'

'I shall do as you say,' Quen replied. 'But what is it I shall find? And what must I do with this thing?'

'You will know what you are looking for,' the woman told him, 'long before you reach the cave. Like the Sacred Eye taken from the cave so long ago, it will be a thing capable of good or evil. We cannot tell you what you must do with it. Whether you bring happiness or destruction to your people and to the forest will depend upon the person you are. That is all I can tell you. Now go with our blessing.'

Although Quen did not fully understand her, he thanked them once again, bowed low, and walked across to the path. At the very edge of the meadow, he turned once and waved, and then set out.

Before long, he had left the last thin remnants of the forest behind and entered the desert – a harsh stony place where nothing lived or grew. He had no fear of the Mollag now, because of what the old man had said about this part of the journey being safe; and without bothering to hide his tracks, he pressed on up the steep hillsides, climbing deeper and deeper into the mountains.

As he wound his way upwards along the stony track, the air became greyer and colder, the clouds above him heavy with unfallen snow, and he was glad of the warm jacket given to him by the woman. At night he pulled the hood up around his face and slept warmly in a cleft between the rocks, while above him the harsh winds of early winter howled between the mountain passes.

It was on that first night that he dreamed the dream. He was alone in a shadowy place, staring into darkness; and slowly, out of the darkness, there appeared a dull red glow which grew steadily brighter until it filled his vision. He stretched his hands forward, wanting more than anything else to reach out and touch the piercing red light; but before he could succeed, he awoke in the grey dawn of a winter morning.

On the following two nights he had the same dream, except that each time it grew more vivid, the red glow seeming to warm him as he slept. And always he awoke with a sense of urgency, wanting to hurry on ever faster up the steepening track.

By the morning of the fourth day he was high in the cold dry mountains. Far below him he could see a solid dark line where the forest began; and looming up ahead, a massive peak of grey rock. On the lower half of the peak was a black gaping hole and he laboured up towards it through the rarefied air. It was, as he suspected, the entrance to the cave, and he crept thankfully inside, out of the cold wind.

Immediately, he found himself in the place of his dream. All around him the rock walls were folded in shadow which swallowed up the faint light from the doorway. And, as if in the distance, he could see a small red glow. Automatically, he moved towards it, slowly at first, then faster and faster until he was running down a long tunnel of rock and shadow; and all the time the red glow grew steadily into a burning fierce red light. His hands were stretched out before him and at last he did what in his dreams had been impossible: he touched the source of this fire – lifted the huge red stone and clasped it to his chest, hugging it as though his very life depended on its warmth and light. As if by instinct, he knew what it was that he held: the Eye of Desire, the one red stone which, secretly, he had been seeking all along. And now, it seemed, nothing else mattered – not the Wise Ones, nor the Mollag, nor the fate of his people in the ten villages. Only this concerned him, this one act of possession.

For a while, he forgot everything – the past and future, even the act of living and breathing. And it was with a sense of surprise that he found himself once more outside the cave, standing in the cold wind beneath the grey brooding peak of sullen rock. The stone was still in his hands and, stowing it carefully in his haversack, he gripped the precious burden tightly and began the descent.

The climb had taken him over three days, but travelling quickly downhill he retraced his steps in less than two. He had no interest in his surroundings any longer. At night he slept curled up around the stone which spread its warmth throughout his body and filled his mind with dreams of fire; and by day, his eyes still dazzled by the visions of red fiery light, he pressed on blindly towards the horizon, looking neither to left nor to right.

Originally, he had intended to stop at the valley and to see the Wise Ones again, to tell them how he had fared on the mountain. But now he passed by the small farm with unseeing eyes, unaware of how the old people paused in their work and watched sadly as he stumbled across the upper edge of the meadow.

Only once during those two days did he stop at all. That was when he became conscious of a steady burning ache in the hollow of his neck. He reached up and felt his diamond glowing and hot within its protective cloth bag, like a warning signal flashing to him through the red fog of madness which had possessed him. But he tore the bag from his neck, impatient and angry, and pushed it roughly into the outside pocket of his jacket where the thick layers of wool shielded him from its white burning light.

The next time he paused was when the fox suddenly appeared on the path before him, its nose raised, snuffing the air, its eyes watching him uncertainly, as though unsure who this person was who had walked out of the past. Quen stared dully at the animal, vaguely conscious of some distant memory which feebly beckoned to him through the glowing red fire that seemed to hedge him in. For a second or two, the boy and the fox faced each other in the dusky late afternoon; then the fox turned and trotted off towards the west, and Quen, after hesitating, stumbled after it. Yet although he followed the bobbing rust-coloured brush as before, he was no longer aware of the animal as another living being. His mind was fixed upon the Eye of Desire, and the faithful animal was merely a useful instrument, a means of finding his way deeper and deeper into his own consuming nightmare of fire.

On the third day, as the old man had warned, the first snow of winter began to fall. The large silky flakes floated down onto Quen, settling in his hair, clinging to the rough surface of his jacket. But he saw nothing: not the gradually whitening world all around him, nor the fire-blackened remains of the forest through which he had once travelled with a sense of grief and shame. The days passed, the snow deepened underfoot, and still it made no difference. He had almost forgotten to eat: he would reach into the haversack for food, his hand would brush the warm smooth surface of the stone, and immediately everything would pass out of his mind. Only fatigue succeeded in thrusting its way through the bewildering red mist. As the light of day faded, he would dimly realize how tired he felt, and he would sink down wherever he was, curling up like some forsaken animal on the surface of the snow, clutching desperately at the stone to warm him through the long, freezing, dream-filled night. Once, the fox crept up to Quen across the frozen crackling snow and made as if to snuggle against the boy for warmth, but the wary creature sensed the presence of the stone and shied away in fear and alarm.

Slowly, the silent pair drew closer to the hills, and as they did so, a disturbing sense of unease gradually broke in upon Quen. This uneasiness increased steadily until one day he looked up and, through a gap in the trees, saw the low hills directly ahead. He knew then what was troubling him. Why am I going there, he wondered. And the answer seemed to flow from the centre of red fire, up through his arms and into his vacant mind. He thought, if I go back there, I might have to give the stone up; or at the very least, I will have to share it. And without a flicker of hesitation he turned away and began travelling towards the north, facing into the cold, deathly wind.

He had ceased eating altogether now, and as one day followed another he became increasingly weak – his body thin and starved, his pale face drawn and haggard, more like the face of a lost ghost than of the healthy boy who had set out for the mountains. Yet still he staggered on, slipping on the icy surfaces of ponds or lakes, pushing his way through deep drifts of clinging snow. Behind him, frightened and bewildered, the faithful fox which had once led the way now followed, limping and footsore, half-dead with hunger. At night, it lay beside the exhausted boy, its fur coated with ice crystals, its meagre body shivering in the gusts of winter wind. And each morning, as the frosty white light lifted the curtain of shadow from the snow, the two of them clambered stiffly to their feet and stumbled on – the fox with its troubled eyes fixed upon the boy; Quen conscious only of the beautiful red fire which glowed between his hands and blotted out the white wasteland through which he stumbled to his death.

In his bewildered state, he did not realize that that was his true destination – his own death somewhere in the frozen wastes of the north. But the fox, practised in the harsh ways of the wild, understood it all too clearly. That was why, when a terrible piercing cry rang out behind them one afternoon, the small animal did not run in fear. It knew that the greatest terror of all lay before them, to the north – and instead, it turned to face the sound of that dreadful cry.

17 · The Awakening

QUEN did not hear the cry at first. Not until it had been repeated several times did it begin to filter through the red mist. It was like an echo from the past, and he stopped and stared back over the way he had come.

He found himself on a flat expanse of ice, in the middle of a frozen lake which was surrounded by leafless trees, their branches heavy with snow. Between himself and the shore there was a rust-coloured patch which he dimly recognized as the fox. And from somewhere close by came repeated cries, both frightening and familiar to him. As he watched, a long thin creature, like something escaped from the night, appeared at the edge of the lake, followed closely by a heavy grey-faced soldier carrying a spear and a club.

There was no possibility of escape. Quen was half-starved and tired – and where could he have run to on this flat icy surface? So he slipped the stone from the haversack and stood clutching it, waiting, as the soldier pushed aside his spidery companion and came lumbering across the ice.

Only the fox stood between Quen and the Mollag, and the brave little animal, weak and cold though it was, held its ground. It flattened itself down onto the ice, ears laid back, teeth showing, snarling and growling at the approaching figure. But the Mollag was not to be stopped by anything so small and insignificant, and when he was still some paces away he flung his spear at the defiant animal. The fox, weakened by its long ordeal, dodged too late, and the metal spearhead sliced along its side, cutting through the fur and skin and grazing the exposed ribs. Unmoved by the blood which poured from the wound, the Mollag ran on across the ice towards the lone boy.

Instead of attacking Quen, however, he stopped a short distance away, his eyes fixed on the stone. It was exactly as if the red glow of the gem were hypnotizing him. Slowly and reluctantly, he fell forward onto his knees and bent his armoured body until his forehead touched the ice in an act of worship.

'Master,' he said hoarsely, 'master.'

Distantly, Quen was aware of what was happening. Somewhere in the back of his mind he understood that his attacker had become his servant – that while he held the stone he was safe. Yet as important as that fact was, somehow he could not concentrate on it. Almost against his will, he found his attention fixed on the crumpled body of the fox. A bloody stream flowed from the fresh wound, forming a large vivid stain of colour on the ice; and at the sight of that warm, living circle of red, the fiery haze or mist which had enclosed him for days parted slightly, enabling him to see clearly. Momentarily, the power of the huge stone passed away from him, and as it did so, the stone itself slipped from his hands and fell onto the snow-covered ice.

He had no chance of retrieving it. Before he could move, the Mollag had leaped forward and snatched it up. The look on his grey lifeless face as he gazed at this unexpected find was something Quen never forgot: his whole expression was one of hideous greed – the mouth sagging open with delight, the moist blue tongue dangling mindlessly from the great opening, the deep-sunken pupils filled with the red reflected glow. With a hoarse cry of greedy joy, the soldier grasped the stone to his chest and turned away. In that instant, Quen and the fox were forgotten, as were his reasons for following them. Leaving the boy where he had found him, the soldier ran back across the ice and into the forest, followed by the Chaser which now let out shrill uncertain cries of protest.

It all took place so quickly that for some time Quen did nothing. Then, as though suddenly realizing what had happened, he too began running towards the trees. But right across his path lay the wounded body of the fox and the widening circle of blood which stained the ice. He knew at a glance that if he deserted the animal it would die; and yet a dull glowing ache within him cried out, urging him to follow the Mollag and retrieve his precious stone. Have I come this far, he asked himself desperately, just to let it slip from my grasp now? For already the calls of the Chaser were becoming faint. And he actually ran past the fox, towards the shore. But before he gained the cover of the trees he stopped again, remembering how he had only been able to come this far because of the fox's help and faithfulness. How could he leave it now to die on the ice alone?

Torn between his two desires – his blind and greedy passion for the stone and the warm bonds of friendship – he sank down onto the snow, his face buried despairingly in his hands. In the distance, he could just hear the faint calls of the Chaser, and nearby the rapid panting of the fox as it fought for its life; and he wanted to cry out in a strange mixture of longing and anger and grief. But before he could open his lips, a moaning gust of icy wind from across the lake blotted out every other sound, lifting the surface snow until it eddied around him in a haze of pure white crystals. Without realizing why, he felt for the hard shape of the diamond, where it nestled still in the pocket of his jacket, and in the brief silence which followed the passage of the wind, he heard his mother's voice speaking to him out of the past: 'the Sacred Eye can be grasped, but never possessed.' The simple force of those words seemed to thrust deep into his mind, clearing the confusion. He looked up and again saw the fox sprawled out in a pool of its own blood – except that now the Mollag and the red stone were forgotten. And with a cry of concern he sprang to his feet and ran back across the ice.

In the cold frosty air, the heavy bleeding had stopped of its own accord, and although the fox was barely conscious, it was still alive. Quen could see that unless it was cared for immediately, given warmth and shelter, it would not survive for long. His first thought was to hold the animal inside his coat and to warm it with his own body – but he soon realized that with the Eye gone, he could not withstand the cold for long himself without fire and shelter. He therefore emptied the haversack, put the fox carefully inside, and carried it across to the trees, where he laid it gently on a layer of thin branches to keep it clear of the snow. Next, he gathered dry twigs and moss from the bark of trees, and with the flint and steel given to him by the Wise Ones, he lit a small fire. Already it was quite late in the afternoon, and Quen quickly collected enough fuel to see them through the night. Then, in the last fading light, and despite his fatigue and weakness, he began digging into the snow, making a shallow hole in which they could shelter from the wind.

By the time he had finished, a wafer of moon had risen above the lake and the stars were showing bright and clear in the black sky overhead. And having eaten some of the dried food and checked to see that the fox was warm and comfortable, he built up the fire and lay down to sleep beside the wounded animal.

Throughout the following day and night, Quen hardly left the fox's side except to gather wood. And on the second morning his vigilance was rewarded, because the tiny animal stirred and half-opened its eyes. Quen was overjoyed, and as soon as the pale wintery sun was shining on the snow, he took the Mollag's fallen spear and used it to make a hole in the ice. Below him, in the grey-blue water, he could see fish lazily swimming to and fro. The problem was how to catch them. Pulling a thread of wool from his tunic, he tied to it one of the dry red berries from the haversack, the brightest he could find. With that as a lure, he crouched beside the hole and, dangling the berry in the water, he waited with spear at the ready.

It was cold frustrating work, and to begin with he missed every fish that came near. But gradually, with practice, he improved, and by the end of the day he had speared two medium-sized fish.

That night the fox woke long enough to take a little of the cooked fish from his fingers. And that, as Quen realized, was the turning point. From then on the small animal improved steadily.

By the fourth day it could crawl from the haversack and stagger across the ice to watch Quen fishing; and by the end of the week it was romping in the snow and eating the fish raw.

Quen had also recovered his strength during that time, and as soon as he was convinced that the fox was fit and well, he set out once more.

There was no chance now of actually following the Mollag – the fresh snowfalls and wind had long since obliterated the tracks. But he reasoned that the Mollag would have to head for the pass in the hills and so he travelled in that direction in the hope of somehow catching up.

Initially, it seemed a very faint hope indeed – for his enemy had a full week's start. But very soon something happened which both puzzled Quen and gave him new heart. They were making their way across a drift of deep snow, Quen sometimes sinking up to his thighs, when the fox suddenly stopped beside a slight depression and sniffed suspiciously. Quen was impatient to hurry on, but he had learned from experience not to ignore these warnings, and he paused and dug carefully down through the snow. He half-expected to find some kind of trap. But he discovered instead the dead body of the Chaser. It had obviously been clubbed to death; and just as obviously, the killer was its Mollag master, because the heavy wooden club, similar to the one which had broken Quen's arm, lay beside the dead body.

For several minutes after making this discovery, Quen sat back on his heels, thinking. Why should the Mollag have destroyed his servant? Quen remembered his own madness when he was carrying the Eye of Desire – he, too, might have done anything during that period. Could it be that the Mollag, crazed by his own greed, had struck out at anything which came near him? Or had the Chaser perhaps tried to take the stone for itself? Whatever the answer, the source of the trouble was clearly the glittering red stone. Nothing else would account for an action as irrational as this. As Faya had warned him long ago, the Mollag were creatures of habit; a soldier would not turn on his own kind unless he was seriously disturbed. But if this particular soldier was out of his mind, what would he have done after the murder? One thing at least was clear: while he carried the red stone, nothing was certain – he might go anywhere, do anything.

Quen stood up and looked uneasily around him. Nothing moved on the white landscape. Even so, when he had covered the dead body once again, he travelled cautiously, peering over every rise before he ventured forward. And throughout that day, and for several more afterwards, he remained always on the alert – shielding the small fires which he lit for warmth and continually scanning the horizon for signs of movement. Yet despite his caution, nothing happened to interrupt or change the course of his journey; and slowly, as he neared the hills, he began to relax. That was why, when the challenge came, he was caught unprepared.

It was a sharp clear morning, the sky grey and overcast, the leafless trees showing gaunt and black against the white glare of the snow. Ever since dawn, Quen had been able to see the faint outline of the hills, but at this point the snow was deep, making walking difficult, so that even after four hours the hills appeared no closer. The fox, forced to wait for Quen who floundered along behind, had soon grown cold and dejected, and for the past hour the boy had carried the animal, holding it inside his jacket to shield it from the wind.

At about mid-morning, he came to what, in summer time, would have been a wide clearing; now it appeared as a large flat expanse of white which offered no cover. Fleetingly, it crossed Quen's mind that it might be wiser to skirt the clearing and keep to the safety of the trees; but on either side the snow had banked up into deep drifts and he finally decided to go straight ahead.

He was half-way across and had just struck a patch of soft sinking snow, when he was alarmed by the reaction of the fox which he still carried. It didn't bark or struggle to escape, but the fur on the back of its neck slowly stood on end. Quen immediately stopped and looked around, hunting vainly for somewhere to hide. And as he stood there undecided, trapped out in the open without cover, the Mollag soldier he was following came bursting out of the woods and ran straight towards him.

It was too late to turn and run, and in the few seconds left to Quen, he pulled the fox out of his jacket and flung it clear. Then he turned and faced his attacker. But even as he planted his feet firmly, bracing himself to meet the rush of that heavy body, he sensed that something was wrong. For one thing, the soldier was unarmed; and instead of running in a direct line, he was wavering and staggering across the snow. The great leather-clad legs moved more and more slowly, the grey three-fingered hands grasping desperately at the empty air. And finally, when he was still yards short of Quen, he stumbled and pitched forward onto his face.

Quen waited, expecting the Mollag to get up; but he remained still and apparently lifeless, stretched out on the snow. Unsure of what was happening, Quen stole cautiously forward and rolled the heavy body over onto its back. It was then, for the first time, that he noticed the gaping wound, an ugly gash just beneath the heart, in a gap between the bronze plates. He also saw, with a faint shock, that the soldier was not quite dead.

His eyes, wide open and staring blindly into space, were flecked with red, as though they were still gazing at the flame-coloured stone which he had taken from Quen. While the boy watched, the great mouth sagged open and the creature gasped out the words:

'My treasure! My treasure!'

The large grey hands lifted slowly, feebly clutching for an invisible object above his head. Only when they encountered nothing did some fearful truth dawn on the Mollag.

'My treasure!' he gasped out once again – and for a moment, an expression of terrible anguish and terrible greed convulsed the features of the face. Then, after a single indrawn breath, the hands fell, the eyes dimmed, and the Mollag died.

Quen, despite his horror of all the Mollag, could not help feeling pity for this poor crazed creature. He had also experienced the power of the red stone and he understood something of what the Mollag must have felt at the end. Moved by an impulse of compassion, he closed the cold grey eyes and was about to fold the deformed hands across the chest, when he was alerted by the fox's bark. He looked up and saw dark figures running through the trees.

This time he was determined not to be caught in the open.

Rolling clear of the dead Mollag, he hurried back across the clearing and scrambled up and over a high bank of snow. He landed amongst the brittle stalks of fern and bramble; and from the comparative safety of that shelter, he turned and looked back towards the distant trees.

18 · The One

QUEN had not long to wait. The two figures he had glimpsed among the trees soon came running out over the clear snow. Even muffled up in heavy winter clothing, there was something familiar about them; but Quen had grown so convinced that nobody except his enemies awaited him in this part of the forest that he failed to recognize them at first. Only when they knelt down beside the dead Mollag and he saw their faces did the truth occur to him. The taller of the two, a lean, strong figure, was none other than Nodak, the woodsman. And the shorter fresh-faced figure, a young girl with light brown hair, was . . .. With a cry of joy and relief, Quen scrambled up over the bank and ran back across the clearing.

'Arla!' he called excitedly, 'Arla!'

His sister looked up, as astonished as he.

'Quen!' she cried, 'Quen! You're safe!'

And she caught him in her arms and hugged him happily.

'But how did you get free?' he asked. 'And what are you doing here? Where did you find Nodak?'

'One question at a time,' she began, laughing, and then suddenly paused as she caught sight of the serious, almost sombre expression on the woodsman's face. 'Nodak, what is it?' she asked urgently.

The woodsman was still kneeling in the snow.

'The Mollag is dead,' he said quietly, his voice fallen to a whisper – and he rose and walked towards the edge of the clearing, where he stopped with his back towards them.

'What's the matter?' Quen asked loudly.

'Hush!' she said, placing her fingers over her brother's mouth. 'He has broken the Law imposed on all who enter Thual.'

'You mean it was Nodak who killed the Mollag?'

She nodded.

'We must leave him alone for a time,' she said. 'It will not be easy for him to accept what he has done.'

While the brother and sister waited, they took shelter from the wind beside the deep snow bank and Arla briefly told Quen how she had come to be there.

It appeared that after Quen's flight from the village, Faya had been captured and locked in the same underground cell as her daughter. With nothing to do but wait, she soon began to worry about her son and to question her wisdom in allowing him to go off into the forest alone. At the first opportunity, she had helped Arla to escape. As it turned out, that had not been particularly difficult – mainly because most of the Mollag were out in the forest hunting for Quen, convinced that he was somehow connected with the treasure they were seeking. Faya herself had insisted on remaining behind, refusing to leave the village while Lod was still imprisoned. But she had instructed Arla to find Quen if he was still alive and to bring him safely back to the village.

'And you see,' Arla cried joyfully when she had finished explaining, 'I have found you, and you're safe and well.'

And she again gave Quen a warm hug.

'But how have you managed to come so far?' Quen asked, thinking of his own slow and hazardous journey.

'Mainly because it's you that they're after,' she said. 'And also because for the past three days I've had Nodak to guide me.'

'But if the Mollag are mainly looking for me,' Quen said, 'why did this one attack you?' – and he pointed towards the cold grey figure in the snow.

'That's one thing I don't understand,' she admitted. 'The few

Mollag I have met, I've easily been able to overcome.' And she fingered the cloth at her neck where, Quen guessed, she carried one of the sacred diamonds. 'But this soldier was different. We discovered his tracks yesterday: they were wandering all over the place, sometimes even in circles, as though he was exhausted or lost. Then, this morning, we found him lying underneath a tree. The moment he saw us he came charging across the snow. We didn't bother to run because I thought I could stop him easily enough.' Here she paused, a puzzled frown puckering her forehead. 'But although I used all my power, it made no difference. Nodak was the one who saved us: he threw his stick and knocked the sword from the Mollag's hand. Yet even that didn't stop him. It was just as though he was mad. He kept shouting something about treasure, and he broke off a heavy branch from a tree and attacked us again. Anything might have happened if Nodak hadn't defended us with the sword. Only when the Mollag had been badly wounded did he run off. And we followed him to here.'

Quen, who had been listening intently, could hardly wait for his sister to finish.

'When you first saw the Mollag,' he said carefully, 'was he carrying anything?'

'No, only his sword.'

'What about the place where you found him? Did he leave anything there?'

'Not that I noticed. As soon as he ran off, we followed.'

'Then we've got to get back to that tree,' Quen said, 'the one he was lying under when you first saw him.'

'But why?'

'There's no time to explain now,' Quen said, and he began running across the snow.

At the edge of the clearing, Nodak turned to face him.

'I cannot go on . . .' he began, but Quen wasn't listening.

'Tell me later,' he shouted, and he hurried away, following the broad tracks made by the Mollag.

They led him straight to a large oak tree, less than half a mile from the clearing. At first it appeared that the Mollag had left nothing behind. But then Quen noticed a hole down near the base of the trunk, roughly covered over with dry branches. He cleared these away and peered inside – and there; nestling in a bed of dry leaves, was the lost stone, its rich colouring casting a deep red glow onto the snow at Quen's feet.

By then, Arla and Nodak had caught up and knelt beside him. He heard his sister's indrawn breath as she saw the stone.

'What is it?' she asked wonderingly.

'It is the Eye of Desire,' he said softly, 'the stone for which I was searching.'

And briefly he told them how he had found and afterwards lost the huge gem.

'Then your journey has been successful,' Arla said, and she reached into the hole in the trunk as though to touch the glowing red surface.

But before her fingers could even brush the stone, her hand began to tremble violently, and she drew back, clutching for reassurance at the diamond which lay concealed in the hollow of her neck.

'I . . . I dare not touch it,' she said slowly. 'It is a fearful thing.'

Watching her, Quen was moved by an impulse to push her aside and grasp the stone himself. But he recognized the feeling for what it was, as the same madness of desire and greed which had possessed him before, and he fought it off.

'Please don't ask me to carry it again,' he said – and he remembered the insane expression on the Mollag's face when he had first scooped up the stone. 'You and Nodak must take it the rest of the way.'

'I can't, Quen,' Arla replied. 'Really I can't. It was you who found it. The Wise Ones put it into your keeping. How can you ask anyone else to carry such a thing?'

As she spoke, she stood up and stepped right away from the tree. Yet Quen could see how attracted she was by the red glow, how she had to struggle against the desire to stoop down and cradle the gem in her arms. Only Nodak appeared unmoved by it, his face still sad and withdrawn, as though a part of him had already wandered off into some unknown region.

'You, Nodak,' Quen said, 'will you take it?'

'I cannot,' the woodsman replied. 'I have broken the Law. I have no place in Thual now. From now on, I belong in the desert regions beyond the forest.'

'But I also broke the Law,' Quen argued, 'and I paid the price. You, too, can make up for what you have done – especially as you were defending Arla.'

'I have done what no human being is permitted to do in Thual,' Nodak said simply. 'I have taken a life. What repayment can there be for that?'

Quen was about to ask him to carry the stone. But before he could speak, the old temptation seemed to reach out and envelop him. Unable to prevent himself, he let his right hand enter the hole and brush the flaming surface of the gem. A tremor of delight and pain passed up his arm, sending red mist swirling into his brain. He looked appealingly at Nodak.

'You must help me get the stone back to the village,' he said.

'Arla is here to do that,' the woodsman replied.

Again Quen's fingers brushed the smooth magical surface.

'But I will need your help too,' he cried desperately. 'I will become like the Mollag. You saw how mad that poor creature had grown.'

Nodak wavered for a moment and then relented.

'Very well,' he said. 'As far as the village. That will be my last duty in Thual.'

'We will both stand by you, Quen, ' Arla added.

But her words went almost unheard, for Quen had already snatched up the stone and was lost in the red mist which blotted out the rest of the world. He knew and cared about only one thing now – the fact that he possessed the Eye of Desire once again. Nothing else seemed to matter.

The journey that day passed unnoticed by Quen. For an indefinite time he seemed to wander through a space lit only by a blinding red light. Arla, Nodak, the fox, these were all forgotten by him. And he only became aware of them again when Arla's insistent voice broke in upon the terrible silence which filled his mind.

'Put the stone down, Quen,' she was saying. 'Put it down' – her voice boring into his consciousness.

With an effort which bordered on physical pain, he let the stone fall, and quickly, before he could retrieve it, Arla covered it with loose earth.

'Now sit here and rest,' she said.

He sank down and found himself in a long, low cave, lit only by a small fire at one end.

'Where are we?' he asked.

Nodak came forward, out of the shadows.

'We are in the tunnel of dark water,' he said. 'Tomorrow, with Arla's power to protect us, we should reach the Caverns. Now we must eat and rest.'

Without argument, Quen ate the food that was given to him, and afterwards curled up on the earth floor. The fox had sidled up to him now that the huge gem was buried, and he could feel the small familiar body against his legs. For further comfort, he slipped his hand inside his tunic and grasped the diamond. It felt tiny after the weight of the red stone; but it sent a warm feeling of peace into his body and limbs, and under its healing influence he fell into a deep and restful sleep.

The next day passed very like the first. Once the burden of the stone filled his hands, he knew nothing except the silent red space which he alone occupied. Somewhere in the background, so distant that he barely noticed them, other things were happening. There was a long rush of cold dark water past his face; the play of bright sunlight on his skin once more; and finally the angry shouts of Mollag guards as Nodak hurried him along the narrow track towards the Caverns. But all these things passed as in a dream. They were somehow unimportant compared with the burning touch of the treasure between his hands. 'My treasure,' he thought repeatedly, 'my treasure' – unaware of how he was echoing the dying Mollag's words.

But again Arla's voice was breaking into the red silence.

'Let go of the stone, Quen; we're here now. Release it.'

With the same wrenching effort, he let the stone fall not into a prepared hole in the earth, but onto a soft cushion.

This time, as the spell left him, he found himself back in the Caverns. He was standing at the end of a large underground hall, on a raised platform, where he had once been questioned by

Alron. Below him, the Pale Keepers were assembled, their eyes fixed on the stone; but now they were not sitting or standing. Instead, all were kneeling, almost as though in prayer. Only Alron was standing erect. Slowly, she moved forward until she was directly below him. Then she raised her hands, joining her fingers to make the sign of the Sacred Eye, and lowered herself stiffly down onto her knees. Immediately, as if by some secret signal, all the Pale Keepers made the same sign, and he heard Alron say:

'It is as we were told: the Wise Ones have sent One to save Thual from the Mollag. You, Quen, are the One. The Master of the Eye.'

19 · Council of War

ALRON'S public statement about his being sent by the Wise Ones was not totally unexpected. What did surprise Quen was the look on the old woman's face and on the faces of the other Pale Keepers. They were only half-watching him: most of their attention was given to the stone which gleamed and sparkled on the cushion. Although nobody moved or came forward, Quen could sense in their watchful gaze traces of the same greed and desire which had consumed the Mollag. And seeing that look again made him feel peculiarly unsafe, even there, in the Caverns, with the great outer door closed on the enemy.

He had the same feeling again that night. He was sleeping in a small room high up in the hillside, the stone locked away in a box which stood in the corner, when suddenly he was woken by the noise of scuffling in the corridor. As he jumped from the bed, he heard Nodak's voice ring out sharply:

'If any of you comes again to this door before morning, Alron shall hear of it.'

There was a sound of receding footsteps and Nodak quietly entered the room.

'You know what they wanted?' he said to Quen.

Quen nodded.

'It is the power of the stone,' he replied. 'Even the Pale Keepers cannot resist it. Only you, Nodak, are unaffected by it.'

But the woodsman shook his head.

'That is not true,' he said. 'Like Arla, I dare not touch it because of what it might do to me. It is a terrible thing: nobody escapes its power. That is why we cannot stay here – even the Caverns are not safe while you carry the great Eye. We must leave soon and take it to the villages where it can do its work.'

'Yes, soon,' Quen said vaguely, and he lay down again on the bed.

Nodak closed the door and Quen heard him stretch out in the corridor, guarding the entrance with his body.

With the woodsman so close at hand, Quen felt reasonably secure, but also wide awake and thoughtful. He knew that what Nodak had said was true: they were not really safe in the Caverns; the Eye tempted all those who saw it. Their best course was to head for the village as soon as possible. Yet Quen quailed before the thought of that journey. And when they reached the villages, what then? The Eye had enormous power, but how was he to use it to defeat the Mollag?

Supposing, for instance, he kept the Eye himself. The Mollag would probably obey him; they might possibly turn against Ungeth. But what would that achieve? Under its evil influence he would be of little use to his people. His own jealousy and greed might well drive him to the point where he became even worse than the Mollag leader.

Then there was also the question of how to keep possession of the stone. He could not carry it with him all the time: its constant touch would drive him mad. No, sooner or later he would have to put it down. Perhaps only for a moment, but that would be enough. That was all the Mollag on the lake had needed – just one unguarded moment. And then what? With the stone in their grasp, the Mollag would be more cruel and brutal than ever; and the suffering of the people would actually be increased.

Lying alone in the darkness, Quen tried to tell himself that there must be a way of using the stone to achieve peace, to drive the Mollag from the land. Yet try as he might, he could think of no workable plan. What had the Wise Ones said to him? 'We cannot tell you what you must do with it. Whether you bring happiness or destruction to your people and to the forest will depend upon the person you are.' The memory of those words placed an enormous responsibility upon Quen. He thought desperately: All this power has been placed in my hands. Somehow I can choose between destroying the villages and saving them. But how?

He didn't sleep for the rest of the night and when dawn came he felt tired and disheartened. He knew that Nodak was expecting him to make a decision, but he remained stubbornly silent throughout the morning. At midday, however, there was again a slight commotion in the corridor, and soon afterwards Arla came to his room.

'Quen!' she said urgently. 'You know we have to leave here soon. Already some of the Pale Keepers are lurking in the corridor asking to be shown the Eye once more. Just its presence here is changing them from friends into untrustworthy servants. If we delay much longer, they may try to prevent our leaving altogether, for fear of losing the Eye.'

Quen shifted uncomfortably on the bed where he was sitting.

'Very well,' he said at last. 'Tell Alron I wish to speak to everyone in the great hall at dusk.'

With that decision made, Quen felt more relaxed, and he slept for most of the afternoon. The light was just fading from the small window high above his head when Arla and Nodak woke him, and clutching the box with the Eye inside, he went down to the hall.

The flares were already lit and everyone was there waiting, as he had requested. Even Namu had arrived for the meeting and was standing at the far end of the hall with the bear at his side. The fox, which had remained close to Quen up until then, stole quietly across to the hairy giant of a man; and Namu, after fondling the small head, smiled at Quen and raised his hand in greeting.

Reluctantly, Quen mounted the platform and faced his audience.

'As you know,' he said nervously, 'my task is somehow to reach the ten villages and to challenge the power of Ungeth.'

He paused, and in the brief silence someone amongst the Pale Keepers called out:

'Why don't you show us the Eye?'

Quen placed his hand firmly on the closed lid of the box.

'That is not why I called you here today,' he said.

Immediately, there was a murmur of discontent amongst the watchers. But Quen refused to be moved by their anger – he knew the dangers of exposing them to the Eye once again. True, it would command their obedience; but it would also increase their greed and make them less trustworthy for what lay ahead.

'Listen to me!' he cried out. 'This is not the time for gazing at the Eye. My duty is to reach the villages. Afterwards, when Ungeth is defeated, you can look as long as you please. But first I need your help.'

Before the audience could show any further signs of unrest, Namu's voice boomed out from the back of the hall.

'What is it you are asking of us, Quen?'

'I'm asking you to help me on the journey itself,' Quen replied, grateful for the interruption. 'The Mollag know that I am here; they may even know of this' – and he lightly touched the top of the box. 'They will therefore be out in force, trying to capture me. What I want you to do is to keep them busy. With Arla and Nodak to protect and guide me, I shall take the most direct route from here to the villages. Your task will be to clear the way ahead of us so that we may travel quickly and in safety.'

He waited, to see what effect his words would have. There was a brief silence, and then Alron slowly rose to her feet.

'What do you propose to do when you face Ungeth?' she asked. It was the same question which Quen had put to himself again and again throughout the previous night. And now, as then, he had no ready reply. For a moment, he thought of telling them the truth, of admitting how frightened and confused he felt – but quickly rejected the idea.

'Do you doubt that I have been sent by the Wise Ones?' he demanded.

The old woman shook her head.

'And do you doubt the power of this?' – again he laid his hand firmly on the box.

'We know that you are the One,' she said, 'and that you have brought the Eye amongst us.'

'Then why do you ask such questions?' he said accusingly. 'When the time comes, I shall do what must be done. You need have no fears about that.'

To his amazement, his reply seemed to satisfy everyone in the hall. Alron, however, had remained standing. Now, she swept her eyes over the audience and turned back towards Quen.

'We agree to help you,' she said deliberately, 'but only on one condition. That when Ungeth is defeated, the Eye of Desire comes back here and remains in our keeping.'

Involuntarily, Quen clutched at the box with both hands, alarmed at the mere thought of losing the stone.

'I cannot agree to that!' he burst out, and then quickly controlled his voice. 'How can I make such a promise?' he went on more reasonably. 'The conflict is not yet over. We have yet to defeat the Mollag. But in the meantime I promise you this: that if we are successful, and I and the stone survive the struggle, I shall return once more to the Caverns.'

'You are playing with words,' Alron said. 'I asked not for your return, but for the return of the stone. You are merely trying to trick us so as to keep the Eye yourself.'

Quen was fully aware of the truth of what she said: he could not bear to think of parting with the Eye. On the other hand, it would have been foolish and dangerous to admit such a thing. As he hesitated, hunting for a reply to her accusation, he had a sudden inspiration.

'Do I have to remind you of the prophecy?' he asked. 'How can I or anyone else keep the stone for himself? We are told by the Wise Ones that it can be grasped but never possessed. If you do not believe that, go beyond the hills and find the Mollag who tried to steal the Eye. He now lies dead in the snow. Is that not proof enough?'

To those who believed in the Law, there was no answer to such a question, and Alron slowly sat down. Nobody else spoke.

'Then we are agreed,' Quen said, gazing around the hall. 'In that case, I give you one hour to clear the Mollag from the track.

By then it will be completely dark and I shall begin the journey to the villages.'

And without giving anyone a chance to reply, he picked up the box and strode from the hall.

In the next hour, waiting up in his room, Quen listened to the bustle below, to the footsteps passing rapidly to and fro along the corridors. The fox had returned to him and lay between his feet, raising its head occasionally to snuff the air, as though it could sense the tense atmosphere in the Caverns. Arla also sat with him in the room, but her eyes were lowered and she said nothing. Quen wondered whether she was as nervous as he during this period of waiting. As on the previous night, Nodak remained outside, guarding the door. But on this occasion nobody came to disturb them.

At the end of the hour, the woodsman opened the door.

'It is time,' he said quietly.

With a strange feeling of desire and dread, Quen grasped the box in both hands and walked out into the corridor. The Caverns now felt deserted, and with Nódak leading the way they hurried towards the main entrance. Alron was waiting there for them, her black robes wrapped around her to protect her from the cold night air.

'The track is cleared,' she said. 'Make good speed.'

Immediately, two Pale Keepers dragged open the heavy door and the cold winter wind blew in upon them. Pulling his hood up over his head, Quen peered out into the night. Already the fox had sidled through the entrance ahead of him – which showed that for the time at least there was nothing to fear.

'To the Hall of Ungeth,' he said in a whisper.

And tightening his hold upon the precious box, he also stepped through the great arched doorway and set out on the final stage of his journey.

20 · Return

WITH the box to shield him from direct contact with the stone, Quen hoped to escape the worst of its numbing influence. Above all, he dreaded falling into that trance-like state which left him more like a restless spirit of the dead than a live human being. As they ran swiftly down the steep track, therefore, he was more intent on observing his own reactions than on looking out for the enemy. And to begin with, it did seem as though he had succeeded in remaining free of that terrible deathly state. For although he instinctively shied away if Arla or Nodak, or even the fox, came too close to him, he did stay reasonably alert. At the bottom of the track, he surveyed the empty tower and the cleared slope as keenly as any of them; and when they ran for the cover of the woods, he made his own way over the uneven, frozen ground and was not led blindly through the darkness.

But as the night wore away, so too did his resistance. It was as if there were something alive within the box which patiently and steadily extended its power over a larger and larger area. Gradually the red mist gathered in Quen's mind, growing ever thicker, more impenetrable. Sometimes it would swirl across his vision, momentarily blocking out the winter scene which surrounded him. And always when his sight came back, it was noticeably dimmer, the shadowy forest further and further away, distanced from him by the swirling red veil. He struggled to retain his grasp upon the present, straining to hear the night sounds, the hooting of an owl or the wind rustling through the bare branches above his head. But despite all his efforts, the sounds and sights of the forest slipped away from him, lost somewhere in the red mist – until all he was conscious of was the hard square of box which he clutched in his hands, and its red glowing centre.

By morning, he had sunk completely into that mindless state of greed and desire which had possessed him earlier. If anything, he was even more lost than before. He failed to hear Arla's voice pleading with him; and when she tried to make him release the box, he fought and kicked, terrified that someone was attempting to steal the Eye.

'Let go! Let go!' he shrieked out, knowing even then that while he held the stone she would have to obey him.

She drew away, head bowed; but still she continued to talk patiently and soothingly to him, until at last he released the box and watched as it was buried in the snow.

Only then did he revive. The red mist cleared and he found they were camped beside a river. On one side, the high bank, eroded by the autumn rains, curved up and over their heads, protecting them not only from snow and wind, but also from the sight of anyone walking above. Quen saw all this at a glance. He was aware also of the anxious faces of his companions watching him. He wanted to say something, to reassure them, but he was too exhausted by his ordeal, and with only a flicker of a smile, he closed his eyes and fell asleep.

Nodak woke him in the afternoon. He sat up and heard in the distance the howling of the wolves and cries of anger and fear.

'It is Namu, clearing Mollag from the trail ahead,' Arla explained quietly. 'As soon as they are driven off, we will go on. But now you must eat.'

And she placed a small heap of dried food in Quen's hands.

He sat there, chewing thoughtfully on the oil-rich nuts, listening to the sounds of conflict fading away into the distance. Arla had said nothing more, yet he could tell that she was impatient to move off. Swallowing the last mouthful of food, he scraped at the snow beside him, revealing the box once more. Immediately, he wanted to reach out and clutch at it; but with a surge of willpower he resisted the temptation. Nodak, he knew, was watching him with a puzzled expression on his face.

'You saw what happened to me last night,' Quen said. 'If the journey goes on like that, I tell you now I shall never reach the villages.'

'But why not?' Arla asked. 'Namu and the Pale Keepers are clearing a path for us; and we are here to help you.'

'I . . . I don't know exactly why,' Quen stammered out. 'Perhaps the power of the stone will grow on me. Perhaps one morning you won't be able to make me release it. I'm not sure. But I can't stand many more nights like that.'

'The boy is right,' Nodak said. 'He was like a mad thing this morning. By tomorrow or the next day he may fall permanently under its spell.'

'Then what are we to do?' Arla asked.

'There are two ways of helping him. The first is to travel in shorter stages. Never to run for more than two hours at a time and to rest in between. That way the journey will be more tiring, but there will be a better chance of Quen's surviving.'

'And the second way?'

The tall woodsman stood up, reached inside his clothing, and drew something out.

'We must give him our own signs, the diamonds which we carry, as extra protection from that thing in the box.'

He opened his clenched fist and revealed a small pale diamond.

'But the Law does not permit that,' Arla protested. 'Nobody may carry the stone of another. The stones themselves will cloud and spoil. You know that.'

'I discovered long ago,' Nodak said, 'that the Law does not apply to Quen as it does to us. When I first came across him injured in the forest, he carried the stone of another – and it was as unclouded then as it is now.'

'But what will protect us when we have given up our stones?' Arla cried, reaching impulsively for the string around her neck.

'Your powers will not leave you for several days,' Nodak said. 'In any case, remember that if Quen fails to reach the coast safely, there will be protection for no one.'

Quen saw the personal struggle pass like a shadow across his sister's face. It was gone from her features in an instant, and she too reached inside her clothing. Without any visible signs of regret, she thrust her hand out towards him, revealing a diamond far bigger than he had expected – a shimmering disc of light almost as large as one of the wild yellow roses which bloomed at the edge of the forest in early summer. He understood then why it was she had returned to the village possessed of such great power, and also why she had managed to survive so easily in the forest when she was searching for him.

'Keep it safely,' she whispered, and turned away.

Quen took both stones and stowed them carefully in the cloth bag which he carried on a string around his neck. Then he stooped and picked up the box which already felt lighter and less burdensome – less of a weight upon his mind and heart.

In the days that followed, Nodak's plan worked well. They travelled only in short, rapid stages with frequent brief rests. And this, together with the power of the three glowing diamonds which hung warm and still against his chest, prevented Quen from falling into the trance-like state. Always, near the end of a run, the red mist would begin to swirl upwards, but never again did he fall entirely under the spell of the Eye.

As Nodak had foretold, the lack of any long periods of rest soon began to tire them out and at the end of every stage he and Arla would lie down in whatever shelter they could find and fall immediately into an exhausted sleep. But Quen, despite his tiredness, found it increasingly difficult to sleep. The question which had troubled him in the Caverns still remained un-answered. How could he possibly use the Eye to defeat Ungeth and his soldiers? And as he drew closer to the villages, that question became more and more pressing.

Even in the few moments when he managed to doze off, he could not escape from it, because it entered his dreams. He would find himself at the end of a long stone-floored hall filled with the Mollag and people from the villages, all of them shouting at him, demanding that he give the Eye only to them. But always his hands were empty, the stone gone, and he would wake up terrified and confused; and in place of those maddened shouts and screams, his mind would be filled with the re-membered advice of the Wise Ones – how the Eye was a thing capable of good or evil; and how the outcome of his journey depended on the person that he was.

Both Arla and Nodak could see how tired and pale he had grown, his face perpetually touched with anxiety, but they could do nothing more to help him. They were not far from the coast now, and the Mollag, mystified by the way the forest dwellers opposed them, were redoubling their efforts to close in on Quen. More and more frequently the three fugitives would meet with injured Pale Keepers or see animals limping away through the undergrowth. And soon it became clear that the final few miles would almost certainly be the most hazardous.

This prospect, too, weighed heavily upon Quen, and during one of their rest periods he actually suggested giving himself up to the Mollag there and then.

'If I surrender,' he said, 'there will be no further loss of life.'

But Nodak would not hear of it.

'We have come too far to give up now,' he said simply.

Quen could not help but agree, and he stood up, ready to set out once again; but Nodak put a detaining hand on his shoulder.

'The time is drawing near,' he said gently, 'and you have told us nothing. What will you do when you reach the Hall of Ungeth?'

Quen was about to avoid the question, as he had done when Alron had challenged him, but he looked at the woodsman, at the steady brown eyes gazing into his own, and he abandoned all thoughts of pretence.

'I'm not sure,' he admitted. 'The Wise Ones would give me no definite instructions. They wouldn't even promise me success. They only said that it was possible for me to bring happiness to the people of the forest – but that destruction was possible too.'

As he finished speaking, he became aware of Arla watching him, her eyes round with astonishment.

'Do you mean to say we're doing all this for nothing?' she burst out. 'That we might all be risking our lives for . . . for failure? After all that's happened, aren't you even sure what you're going to do?'

'I shall know when the time comes,' Quen replied stubbornly. 'When I'm face to face with Ungeth I shall do what is necessary.'

'And do you think that's guarantee enough . . . ?' she began, but Nodak cut her short.

'No part of this journey has been based on careful plans or knowledge of what lay ahead,' he said. 'Faya had only the vaguest idea of what she was asking Quen to do, yet still she sent him. And even though Quen was told that the Wise Ones and the Eye did not exist, he continued to search. It was trust, not knowledge, which saw him through. And we must rely on that same trust now.'

Quen already had a lot to thank Nodak for, but never had he felt quite so grateful. For not only had the woodsman cut short Arla's accusations; his words also renewed Quen's failing courage, reminded him of how, against all odds, he had succeeded so far. And when they rose to move off, he was filled with some of his old hope and determination.

In view of what happened soon afterwards, that was just as well. All that morning the forest had seemed restless and troubled, with sounds of shouting and conflict never far distant. At every turn of the path they half-expected to meet danger. So that when it actually did occur, it was not really a surprise. They had forded a shallow stream and were climbing up the opposite bank, when the bushes ahead of them parted and revealed two Mollag soldiers.

Arla was the first to act. She leapt in front of Quen, and immediately the two soldiers were frozen into stillness.

'Don't waste time,' she whispered fiercely. 'I can hold them long enough for you to escape.'

Before Quen could argue or hesitate, Nodak had dragged him up the bank and back into the cover of the forest. But they had not gone far before their way was again blocked by soldiers. Pushing Quen to one side, Nodak raised the stick which he carried, balancing it in his hand.

'The village is close now,' he said quietly. 'You must finish your journey as you began it – alone.'

And as the soldiers charged across the narrow clearing towards Nodak, Quen slipped between the trees and ran swiftly across the snow-covered ground.

21 · The Hall of Ungeth

QUEN was not totally alone as Nodak had said. The fox was still with him, and once again he followed the red-brown brush as it bobbed and weaved its way across the snow. Like Quen, the tiny animal knew there was no point in hiding or backtracking now: there were enemies on every side and they were leaving behind them a trail which could not be mistaken. Their only safety lay in speed and so they ran directly towards the west, ignoring the paths which curved away on either side, crashing their way straight through the dry underbrush and snow.

In less than an hour the forest grew noticeably thinner and more than once he saw the stumps of felled trees which told him clearly that he was close to the village. He paused and looked around him. All sounds of conflict had disappeared and the forest was unnaturally still, not even a breeze stirring the black leafless branches. Nearby was a tall ancient tree, half-dead down one side; and placing the box gently on the snow near its base, Quen slowly began to climb.

The bark of the tree was brittle and, in places, encrusted with snow and ice, which meant that he had to move carefully. But gradually he worked his way upwards, until eventually he was high enough to see over most of the surrounding trees. As he suspected, the edge of the forest was less than a mile away: he could see the tall sinister towers of the Mollag and, beyond them, the huts of his own village. Now, it seemed, the moment of decision had come, and as he climbed down he tried desperately to think of some plan, some way of using the stone which he had brought so far. With one part of his mind he wanted above all else to help the villagers; but still, behind that wish, lurked his own selfish desire, his fear that the Eye might pass out of his hands.

As he reached the ground, however, all thought of this problem was driven from his mind by the sight of the fox which was standing stock-still and alert, staring back over the way they had come. Quen followed the direction of the fox's gaze, but for a moment he could see nothing unusual. Then there was a slight movement between the trees and he made out the unmistakable outline of a Mollag, the heavy face thrust forward, studying the ground. As yet, they had not been seen, and picking up the box Quen darted off in the direction of the village; but within ten paces there was a hoarse shout from behind, followed by the sound of a heavy body crashing along in pursuit.

Quen had no doubt that he could reach the village ahead of the Mollag. Yet what would be the use of that if he still had no clear idea of how best to use the Eye? More than ever before, he needed time, time to stop and consider his position. But with the Mollag close behind him that was out of the question. Think! think! he told himself as he laboured through the snow. And all at once he saw clearly that the only thing he could possibly do now was to hide the Eye somewhere while he worked out a plan. But how could he hide it here, so close to the towers? If he placed it in a tree, with no leaves to protect it, it would be clearly visible from below; and if he buried it in the snow, his tracks would lead the Mollag directly to the place. Then where?

All of this passed through his mind in a flash. Never once did he pause or look back. The fox was still bounding along before him and he was running down a path flanked on either side by a tangle of dry ferns which poked up through the unblemished snow. Ahead of him, already visible through the trees, was the tall outline of a tower. There was no opportunity left to seek out a safe place, and as he passed a huge growth of green holly which clung to a dying oak, he flung the box far to his left.

It curved away from him, spinning in the cold air, and then fell, breaking through the crust of snow without a sound and disappearing in amongst the dry stalks of fern. From the path, the hole which it made in the snow was barely visible. Even to searching eyes it looked no more than a shadow or slight depression. And satisfied that it was safe for the time, Quen, who had hardly paused in his stride, hurried on.

Now the edge of the forest was directly in front of him. The fox had stopped and turned to face him, unwilling to venture out into the open, perhaps sensing that this was the end of the journey; and Quen, unable to stop, leaped over his small companion and broke from the cover of the trees, out onto the farmland which bordered the forest.

Not far away there was a group of villagers carrying heavy bundles of dry wood and he ran straight towards them for help. Only when he was right up to them did he realize that it was a line of prisoners and that they were chained together. There was a murmur of surprise as he sank down, breathless, before them. He heard a friendly voice say:

'I think it's young Quen.'

And then somebody gripped him by the shoulders and he found himself staring into his father's face.

'Quen!' Lod burst out. 'Thank heavens you're safe!'

But before he could reply, the guard in charge of the prisoners had pushed Lod roughly aside and had grasped Quen by the hair, forcing him to his feet. Moments later, the Mollag who had been chasing him came charging across the ploughed field.

'You will run no more,' he said angrily, and twisting Quen's arm behind his back, he marched him towards the nearest tower.

From somewhere behind him, Quen heard Lod call out:

'Did you find it, Quen? The Sacred Eye, have you brought it back?'

'It's safe . . .' he began, but before he could finish, the Mollag had slapped him across the side of the head.

'You will speak only when you are told to,' he commanded, twisting Quen's arm even further up his back.

In silence, Quen was led to the tower. Beneath it was a trap-door and a ladder down which he was made to climb. Below ground, there was very little light, but as he was pushed or dragged along, he had the impression of being in a damp, rocky tunnel. Occasionally, a chink of grey winter light showed through from an air vent above; and it was near one of these vents that the Mollag finally stopped and lowered him down into a pit.

'I have to see Ungeth,' he shouted.

But the only reply he received was the creak of leather as the Mollag walked away.

It took him only a few minutes to discover that escape from the pit was impossible. He could not reach to the top, and the sides were made of smooth stone which offered him neither hand- nor foothold. There was nothing to do but wait, and he sat down on the cold stone floor and tried to puzzle out what he should do when and if he was brought before Ungeth. Yet although he tried hard to think, always his mind was drawn back to the image of the box with its secret glowing centre – somewhere out there, buried in the snow. A thing capable of good or evil, the Wise Ones had said. And gradually, in spite of his strong desire to hold it once more and never again let it slip from his grasp, the conviction grew on him that the Eye was above all a thing of evil, something called into being by the presence of the Mollag.

Slowly, the day wore on and the chink of light far above him faded into night as the early winter dusk fell. Soon he was in total darkness and, assuming that he would be left there for the night, he curled up and tried to sleep. But he had barely closed his eyes when he again heard the creak of leather in the passage and a knotted rope was tossed down to him. He swarmed up it and the icy fingers of a Mollag guard closed on his wrist once more, pushing him forward into the darkness.

This time they didn't travel very far. He was made to climb down a ladder to a deeper level where their way seemed to be blocked by a solid slab of rock. But the guard leaned against it and it slid open, revealing a huge underground cavern or hall, lit by bluish-grey flares. Quen was standing at the head of a flight of steps, with the hall below him, its patterned flagstone floor stretching away to a large raised chair or throne at the far end.

At first, he thought it was empty; but then a slight movement caught his eye and he suddenly realized that the walls were lined with Mollag guards, their skins almost invisible, like deathly streaks of shadow in the bluish-grey light. As he watched, others entered the hall from the far end: figures he knew – many of the Pale Keepers, Faya and Lod, Namu, Arla and Nodak, even the withered body of old Alron. Most of the Pale Keepers were wounded (which explained their being captured) and all who possessed the power of the Eye wore blindfolds. Very few, it seemed, had escaped Ungeth's net; and confronted by all these familiar faces, Quen understood why he had been made to wait for so long in the pit. Clearly, Ungeth wished to emphasize the extent of his success and of Quen's failure.

At a sign from the guard, Quen descended the steps and walked towards his friends. He began to call out to his mother and father, but again the guard slapped him across the head.

'There will be no talk amongst you,' he said.

And in silence they waited as a door beside the throne opened.

Quen expected another Mollag to appear, a figure larger and more hideous than any he had seen. But instead, a tall man stepped through the opening. He had soft brown hair and handsome features and was dressed in a gold- and silver-coloured robe. Quen would never have associated him with the Mollag if it had not been for his eyes. They alone gave him away – grey and steel-hard, without depth or feeling.

Before he could prevent himself, Quen broke out:

'But you're a man!'

The handsome face smiled without humour, the eyes unchanging.

'Why should I be otherwise?' he asked.

'Because of the Mollag. You're their master.'

'And are the Mollag so very different from men?' Ungeth asked sarcastically. 'They too are driven by greed and hunger. Perhaps simpler than men, but not so very different.'

For some reason, Ungeth's words recalled to him the story told by the Wise Ones – how once, long ago, the greedy desires of the people in the forest had threatened to bring destruction on both themselves and Thual. And yet that was only one story.

What of the other, happier stories told to him by his mother?

'Yes, sometimes men are driven by greed and hunger,' he said. 'But that doesn't make them exactly like the Mollag. They have other feelings as well, better feelings, which . . ..'

But Ungeth cut him short.

'I did not bring you here to argue with me,' he said coldly. 'You know what I want of you – though why it should be placed in the keeping of a boy, I shall never understand.'

'I don't know what you're talking about,' Quen replied, pretending ignorance.

'Don't lie to me, child,' Ungeth said. 'I came here because I heard stories of a treasure – a huge gem, bigger than a man's two fists, perfect and without flaw. Obviously you do not carry it with you now. But somewhere close by, you have it hidden. I am sure of that. What other reason would all these people have for protecting you so bravely?' He gestured gracefully towards the rest of the assembly. 'They represent the power of Thual and of the ten villages. They would not risk life and freedom for a mere boy without good reason.'

Quen realized immediately that there was little to be gained by lying.

'Supposing such a stone exists,' he said, 'do you think I would simply bring it here and place it in your hands?'

'Ah, I see you are not a fool,' Ungeth said, again smiling humourlessly. 'You understand that everything must be paid for. Very well, what price do you place upon this gem?'

Quen hesitated. He knew that, if necessary, Ungeth could probably force the truth from him by torture. And although he still yearned to keep the stone for himself, he continued to feel, as he had done earlier in the day, that it was an evil thing, sure to bring harm on all who fell under its influence.

'The price . . .' he began.

But before he could go on, Faya, who had somehow managed to free her hands, tore the blindfold from her face. One of the guards stepped forward, but Ungeth waved him back.

'Don't listen to him, Quen,' she cried. 'The Eye has no price. If you give it up to him, you will betray us all.'

'Be silent, woman!' Ungeth ordered – and then, nodding towards Quen: 'Go on.'

'The price I ask is this,' Quen said, 'that you and your Mollag board your ships immediately and leave this coast forever.'

There was a pause, everybody watching the Mollag leader.

'Unfortunately,' he said at last, 'your price is too high. Now let me tell you what I am prepared to pay. From this moment, you are free to leave – to go back to your village, to the forest, wherever you please. No one will threaten you or follow you or force you to return. But unless the gem is here in my possession by one hour after dawn tomorrow, all of these people, all of your friends and helpers, will die. Is that understood?'

Almost before he had finished speaking, Faya darted forward and grasped her son's hands.

'Don't pay his price!' she cried out. 'No matter what he asks, keep the Eye safe. By giving it up, you will place a curse on the land forever.'

'Silence her!' Ungeth shouted, and a guard dragged her to the side of the hall and put a cold shadowy hand over her mouth.

'I ask you again,' Ungeth said, 'do you understand my terms?'

Quen nodded dumbly.

'And do you agree to them?'

Quen glanced at his mother, and then at the ring of watching or listening faces. There was a terrible stillness in the hall, broken only by the splutter of flares around the walls.

'Yes,' he said at last, 'I agree.'

22 · Sacrifice

WHEN Quen emerged from the underground tunnel, it was late and cold, with a thin white mist hanging in the night air. As Ungeth had promised, nobody followed or challenged him, and he walked across the frozen furrows of the open farmland towards the village. A Mollag soldier was standing guard near the outer ring of dwellings, but he said nothing as Quen approached – merely peered through the mist to see who it was, and then paced off slowly into the darkness.

Nothing had changed while he had been away – perhaps the round mud-walled huts appeared slightly smaller, but that was all. He stopped beside what had once been his home, the hut he was born and raised in, and ducked through the low doorway. Inside, it smelled musty and unused, proof of how long it had stood empty. Groping along the shelf, he found the flint and lit a small dish-lamp which always stood close to the hearth. The open flame sputtered and grew, revealing the familiar walls and floor, the four narrow beds still heaped with dead rushes; but deserted like this, it no longer felt like home. The kindling in the hearth was wet, the bedding sodden, and when he touched the wall beside his head, it felt clammy and damp. Tired and downhearted as he was, this was no place to take refuge in – barely a refuge at all. Yet where else was there for him to go?

With a sigh, he sat down on the edge of one of the beds and stared gloomily at the open doorway. Somewhere out there in the darkness, the Eye, lying protected in its box, awaited him. In some ways he longed to hold it again, to feel its weight between his hands. Yet what was the point? He knew that the longer he had it in his possession, the harder it would be to give up. And there was no doubt now that it had to be given up to Ungeth. Although it still attracted him, made him yearn to possess it, he no longer revered it as Faya did. He had seen its beauty, its pure red light; but he had experienced the evil which the Wise Ones had referred to – the way it destroyed the mind and judgment and reduced people to blind, murderous slaves.

He would willingly have given it up – if, by so doing, he could have rid the land of the Mollag. What angered him was the thought of simply handing it to Ungeth. True, he would be saving many lives. But in the end everything would be as it was before and his journey would all have been for nothing. Or perhaps, what was worse, conditions in the villages might grow even more intolerable. As the Eye exerted its terrible power over Ungeth's mind, there was no knowing what he might make the Mollag do to the people.

The more Quen thought about such things, the more gloomy he became; and in order to comfort himself, he took the three diamonds from the cloth bag around his neck and placed them carefully in the dust at his feet. Even in the weak uncertain flame of the lamp, they sparkled and shone, gathering into a single liquid pool of bluish light which seemed to draw him in. He was unaware of what was happening at first: the mud walls of the hut wavered and disappeared; there was a period of strange silence during which he again felt as though he were drifting down through sun-drenched water; and suddenly, in a moment of brilliant vision, he found himself in another time and place. Although he didn't realize it, it was very similar to his experience in the Caverns, in the Chamber of the Eye, when he had caught brief glimpses of the future – except that this time he was transported back into the distant past, to something which had happened long before he was born.

He found himself watching a young man who was climbing up

a steep hillside. Although Quen had never seen him before, there was something familiar about him, and somehow Quen knew that he was the one who had first gone to the Wise Ones and brought the Sacred Eye of Seeing back to Thual. The Eye itself was clutched in his hands, a great brilliant globe of light which stood out against the barren hillside. At the top of the hill the young man turned and held the Eye out before him. Far below, the valley ended in a tumble of rocks; and somewhere in the background, people were moaning with distress and anger. Nobody moved. The scene was absolutely still. But its meaning, to Quen, was clear enough, and with a cry of dismay he awoke.

He was back once again in the mud hut. Everything looked as it had before. The mud walls were streaked with damp; a thin blanket of mist drifted in through the low doorway; outside, the Mollag guard paced slowly past. But now everything appeared different to Quen, less dreary and hopeless, because finally he knew what had to be done. His only remaining doubt was in himself – whether he would possess the strength of will to carry the action through to the end. Yet, whatever the cost, he must; there would be no second chance.

With a sudden sense of determination, he went to the doorway and peered outside. Already the night was far advanced, and he needed all the rest he could get for what lay ahead. Scooping up the diamonds, he lay down on the earth floor; and before the guard again passed the hut, he had fallen into a deep restful sleep.

He awoke, as always, at dawn, when the first grey light began filling the hut. He felt cold and hungry; but there was no food on the shelves and the kindling was too wet to make a fire. In any case, he had no time to waste and he was frightened of what he might do if he once paused to consider what awaited him. So pulling his hood up over his head, he left the hut immediately and ran stiffly across the hard crust of snow towards the forest.

As before, the guards on the ground and in the towers ignored him and he quickly found the path he had used the day before. Even his own footprints and those of the Mollag were still visible, and he followed them back as far as the tall growth of holly. From there, he waded through the snow and dried ferns towards the small square hole which, in the early light, showed as little more than a fragment of shadow. The box was still there, where it had landed, and he picked it up and wiped the dry snow from its sides. He was tempted to open the lid, if only for a moment, in order to see the stone once more and to touch it lightly with his fingers. Already he could feel its warmth seeping through into his hands and arms. But he knew how dangerous even a glimpse of it might be and, tucking the box under his arm, he hurried back along the path.

The sun had risen when he reached the tower and was showing as a hazy yellow-white disc above a low bank of cloud. Quen looked at it for a moment, almost longingly, and then climbed down into the darkness. A guard was waiting for him and, as before, he was led along the tunnel and down to the entrance of the hall.

When the door swung open and he stepped forward to the head of the steps, he found that everybody was already there, waiting: his family and friends, even Ungeth, who was pacing impatiently before his throne. It looked, at first, exactly like the scene he had left the night before. But as his eyes became accustomed to the bluish light, he noticed that the Mollag guard was far stronger than it had been. Instead of the single line of soldiers, they now stood three or four deep along the walls. Clearly, Ungeth meant it as a warning, as a show of strength; but to Quen, the rows of shadowy figures were a strangely heartening sight, more than he had dared hope for.

'I see you have agreed to my price,' Ungeth called out, and motioned him forward.

But instead of descending the steps, Quen placed the box at his feet and loosened the catch.

'Before I show you the stone,' he said, 'I must ask one thing of you. Let me have more witnesses among my own people for what I'm about to do.'

'I'm not a fool,' Ungeth said harshly. 'I'm aware of what might happen if all the blindfolds were taken off.'

'This is no trick,' Quen replied. 'Two further witnesses is all I ask – the old woman, Alron, and my mother.'

Ungeth nodded to one of the guards and the two blindfolds were removed.

'You do not need me as a witness, Quen,' Faya called out. 'You know that what you are doing is betrayal, without my eyes to tell you so.'

'Let your own eyes be the judge,' Quen called back, 'for what you are about to see is the thing you prize above your own safety. Look at it carefully, and then tell me if you think it is worth the price of life and freedom.'

And throwing back the lid of the box, Quen grasped the stone and held it high above his head. There was a gasp of amazement from everyone watching.

'It is the treasure!' Ungeth cried out, starting forward – while all around the hall the guards stirred restlessly, their eyes gleaming red with growing desire. 'It is the treasure!' Ungeth cried again, his voice risen almost to a shriek. 'The thing for which I've searched so long. Give it to me, boy.'

But Quen did not move. The stone felt as though it were burning into his hands and he sensed immediately the danger he was in. Red flames seemed to be flickering up, threatening to engulf him – yet somehow he knew that he must hold it long enough for it to do its work.

Ungeth had leaped down from his throne and was shouting incoherently. But his voice was almost drowned out by the growing roar from the Mollag. They had pushed in from the walls, eyes gleaming greedily, and were moving slowly towards the steps. Soon, only a narrow strip of stone floor remained between the bottom of the steps and the advancing crowd.

'The stone is mine!' Ungeth screamed, fighting his way through the throng. 'Remember your promise, boy!'

But before he could reach the steps, Quen's voice rose above the general noise.

'Get back! All of you! Obey the bearer of the stone!'

Immediately, the shouting dwindled to a murmur, and then to silence. And slowly, one by one, the Mollag fell to their knees in an act of worship. Finally, only Ungeth was left standing; and reluctantly he too slumped forward onto his knees.

In the heavy silence, no one moved. And Quen, almost blinded by the red light which seemed to pulse from the stone, thought: Now! now is the time!

148

'Here, before you,' he said deliberately, forcing himself to mouth the words, 'is the treasure you have come for.'

And with a supreme effort he drew back his arms and steeled himself to break the bond which held him to the stone. Yet although he strained, exerting all his will, nothing happened. His body remained arched, his arms rigid. It was as if the stone were glued to his hands, fastened there by some invisible power. And in a flash of despair, Quen imagined that he was again lost in the snow, wandering towards the frozen horizon forever.

That vision lasted only for a moment. Instantly, he was aware once again of the crowded hall, the kneeling figures, the upturned faces. But now he knew that all his hopes had been foolish. He would never give up the stone. Never. No matter what the cost. He would rather accept this grisly kingdom – rule over the hated Mollag – suppress and enslave his own people. Anything rather than lose the stone.

'Curse you, Ungeth!' he called out. 'Curse you!'

But neither that cry, nor his own despair, nor the knowledge of his failure made any difference. He would do whatever was necessary to keep the stone, even take over Ungeth's power – the very power he had striven so hard to destroy.

Stooping down, he thrust the stone into the protection of the box, already beginning to feel jealous of the many eyes which gazed greedily at it – aware too of how dangerous it was to allow others to stare at it for a long period. For the time being, he thought, there was nothing to fear.

But he had forgotten the guard who had brought him to the hall and who still waited silently behind him. As Quen's fingers released the precious jewel, this guard pushed past him and plucked it from the box. With a roar of delight, he clutched it tightly in both hands. But only for a second or two. Quen, freed of the terrible weight of the stone, saw one last opportunity before him. And slipping the knife from the side of his boot, he sliced through the grey skin on the back of the Mollag's hand with the thin blade. The guard, recoiling instinctively from the pain, released his hold on the Eye, and as it slid from his fingers, Quen caught it in one hand and hurled it down towards the stone floor.

Below him, there was a rush of bodies trying to save it. But too late. The perfect red gem clipped the edge of the bottom step and shattered into a thousand pieces which rolled and bounced beneath the feet of the advancing crowd.

It was impossible to follow clearly what happened after that. Almost immediately, the crowd became a dangerous, snarling mob. Swords were drawn, spears raised, as the Mollag fought for the shining red fragments which strewed the patterned floor. There were cries of rage and pain, shrieks of joy and despair, and somewhere in the midst of it all, Ungeth, alone and unarmed, being cut down by his own guard. Quen saw the handsome head with its cold eyes disappear amongst a surging mass of struggling bodies, and then he too was pushed backwards. But not down beneath the trampling feet and clash of weapons. He staggered back and fell against the tall stone door which immediately swung open behind him; and all at once he was standing out in the deserted tunnel with Nodak beside him.

'Namu is leading the others out by the far door,' the woodsman said. 'They will be safe now. Alron and Faya have sent me to make sure you escape.'

'Then they don't think . . . ?' Quen began, and stopped, for he could already see the answer in Nodak's eyes.

'They have seen,' the woodsman said simply. 'They no longer doubt the messenger of the Wise Ones.'

And taking Quen by the hand, he led him along the dark tunnel and up into the clean yellow sunlight.

23 · Reward

THE FIGHTING below ground went on for three days, and during that time the people cowered in their huts or took refuge in the fringes of the forest. Late on the second morning the confused noise of battle seemed to reach its height, and thereafter began to die down slowly, until by the following morning it was little more than a murmur. Soon afterwards, on the afternoon of the third day, the surviving Mollag, greedily clutching fragments of the Eye, left the tunnels and made their way down to the boats. Most of them were wounded, many of them badly, and yet they still fought, soldier hacking at soldier, dying cries coming from the long ships which wallowed in the deep water beyond the breakers.

By nightfall, all the ships had gone, but the villagers stayed in hiding, fearful that they might return. The horizon, however, remained empty. Occasionally a deserted wreck was washed ashore, but that was all. And gradually, as the days passed, the people emerged – nervously at first, and then with growing confidence.

What they found was chilling enough: the tunnels choked with dead; the shoreline littered with those who had failed to reach the ships. It seemed unlikely that many of the Mollag could have escaped; and those few had probably destroyed each other out at sea. Of the fragments of red stone, there was no sign. Not even the tiniest splinter remained – all had been carried greedily down to the ships and now lay somewhere at the bottom of the ocean, lost forever.

In the weeks that followed there was a great deal for the villagers to do. Working in teams, they wiped out every trace of the Mollag. They brought rocks from the distant headlands and filled in the underground tunnels. The towers were dragged down and chopped into huge piles of kindling. And the great storage bins which the Mollag had sunk in the earth were broken open and the food carried back to the villages.

Throughout this time of activity, Quen often looked with longing eyes at the forest; and more than once, when he was chopping wood in the fading evening light, he heard the nearby bushes rustle and he thought he caught a glimpse of the sharp, pointed nose of the fox. But there was so much for everyone to do at that stage that he had no time to stand thinking about the past. Also, his parents and sister were so pleased to have him back that he didn't have the heart to tell them how closed in and dull he found life in the village, nor how much he missed the broad reaches of the forest.

Not until early spring did village existence get back to normal, and now, at last, Quen had more leisure. He was, understandably, something of a hero amongst the people and, despite his age, was already treated as a man. Yet even that didn't make up for what he felt he had lost. Whenever he had the chance, he would walk off alone and think regretfully of the past – of his many adventures; of Namu and Nodak who had gone with the Pale Keepers to destroy the towers in the forest; of the small fox which had served him so faithfully; and of the Wise Ones and their simple farm on the fringes of the desert. Already, those friends and experiences seemed far off, as though gone forever; and never a day passed without Quen sighing unhappily for what he would never have again.

It was on just such a day, mid-way through the spring, that Quen was startled by the sound of shouting and cheering. He had been sitting gloomily in the hut, thinking as always of the past, and curious to discover what was happening, he got up and went outside. To his amazement, hundreds of people from all the villages were gathered on the open farmland; and slowly walking over from the forest were Nodak, Namu, and a group of Pale Keepers carrying Alron in a covered litter.

Unsure of what was happening, Quen ran to the edge of the crowd, hoping for a better view. But no sooner was he noticed than he was hoisted onto the shoulders of some young men and borne triumphantly to the centre of the gathering. A small wooden platform had been erected and he was lifted onto this while all around him people were laughing and clapping and chanting his name. The noise did not stop until Alron stepped down from the litter and held up her hand – then, within moments there was silence.

'You all know why we are here,' she began. 'Partly to celebrate the defeat of the Mollag; but also, and just as important, to thank Quen for what he has done. I have no doubt that in years to come his story will be told and retold throughout the ten villages, and so he needs no further praise from an old woman like me. What I bring him instead is a gift. Not just an ordinary present, but something of far greater value – the gift of choice.' Here she turned to face Quen himself. 'You have been brought up in the villages;' she went on, 'you have travelled throughout Thual; you alone have spoken to the Wise Ones and climbed the mountains of the desert. Of all the many things you have seen, what do you most desire? For if it is in my power to give, it shall be yours.'

Quen looked round at all the expectant faces and back towards Alron. Although he had never dreamed of such a moment, he knew straight away, without a trace of doubt, what he must ask for.

'It's true I have seen many things,' he said, 'but none of them more exciting and wonderful than Thual itself. Long ago Nodak told me that without Thual there would be nothing. I didn't know what he meant at the time; but since then I've seen the desert lands, where nothing lives or moves, and now I understand. That's why I only have one request: I wish to become a woodsman and spend the rest of my life in the forest.'

As he finished speaking, Quen glanced across to where Arla

and his parents were standing, uncertain of how they would take his request. It had crossed his mind that they might feel deserted by him. But they smiled back happily, proud of the way he had answered.

Alron also smiled and turned towards Nodak.

'What do you say to such a request?' she asked him.

Nodak stepped up to the platform, his face as stern and serious as when Quen had last seen him.

'As you know,' he said, 'I have broken the Law of Thual and must leave the forest now that peace has come. Therefore it is good that Quen should wish to become a woodsman, to take my place.'

'But how can I learn the ways of the forest on my own?' Quen burst out. 'I need someone to teach me, someone who knows the trees and plants and rivers, everything.'

'It is true what the boy says,' Alron added.

'Please, Nodak,' Quen said. 'I couldn't learn without you there.'

The tall woodsman stared thoughtfully at the ground for some time before looking up.

'We all have much to thank Quen for,' he said at last. 'Even Thual itself owes him a debt. And if by remaining in the forest I can repay some of that debt, then I shall gladly stay.'

Immediately a great cheer went up from the waiting crowd and Quen laughed happily. As the noise died down, Alron called out:

'And so that is your only request, Quen?'

Quen hesitated and looked towards the tall silent figure of Namu.

'There is only one thing,' he began, but the big man, as if reading his mind, held up his hand for silence.

'Since winter,' he said slowly, 'the fox has haunted the edge of the forest, waiting for his companion.'

He pointed towards Thual, and whether it was the breeze or something moving in the bushes, nobody was sure – though some of the villagers claimed to have seen a small rust-coloured body sliding away through the spring growth.

'Then your choice is made,' Alron said solemnly, and led the way to the village where a feast of celebration had been prepared.

It went on for three whole days, with everyone singing and dancing. But the people of the forest left early on the second morning, and Quen was amongst them.

As for the rest, the years that followed – he had many more adventures. In the villages there is still a great deal of talk about him: some say that he somehow won for himself the biggest of all the diamonds in the Chamber of the Eye; while others claim that he succeeded in finding the Wise Ones yet again and revisiting the cave in the mountains. But that, of course, is another story.